MURDER
at
WALDEN POND

A Steve Asher Mystery

MURDER
at
WALDEN POND

A Steve Asher Mystery

AL BLANCHARD

SALVO PRESS
Bend, Oregon

MURDER at WALDEN POND

Copyright © 2001 by Al Blanchard

Salvo Press • P.O. Box 9095 • Bend, OR 97708
www.salvopress.com

Library of Congress Control Number: 2001088847

ISBN: 1-930486-28-6

Printed in U.S.A.
First Edition

To Enid,
Your love and friendship inspires.

PROLOGUE

A conference about one of my students at seven-thirty in the evening was unusual, but Susan Oliver had made it sound urgent.

I pushed open the door to Wilson's diner. The aroma of freshly perked coffee mixed with cigarette smoke. Susan was sitting in the last booth on the left. I had seen her at school a few times, but as I slid into the booth I was struck by how attractive she was.

"Thanks for meeting me this late, Mr. Asher," she said.

"Please call me Steve."

She squinted and smiled. "Thirty-four, right? I'm good at guessing ages."

"Not bad," I said. "Thirty-five. I've been thirty-five for four years now."

"That makes you eleven years older than me."

The waitress arrived and we ordered coffee. Susan's blonde hair fell to her shoulders and her blue sweater matched her eyes. She didn't wear a trace of make-up.

She had called me at school to set up an appointment to talk about her brother, Petey. He'd been getting into trouble lately. I was his eighth grade U.S. History teacher.

"I can't seem to get through to him," she said. "Ever since Dad walked out on us a few years ago Petey and I haven't gotten along. I work odd hours and I'm not around a lot. I just want to know how to help him get through this. Mom's been sick lately and had to stop working. She tries to control him, but he just can't seem to sit still."

"Petey's really bright and that's part of what gets him into trouble," I said. "I've never seen a kid work harder if he thinks something is worthwhile. The trick is to show him how important school is."

We sipped our coffee and talked for about ten minutes. Then I said, "I got the feeling on the phone that something was bothering you besides Petey's school work."

"Can I talk to you confidentially?"

"Sure."

"I think Petey's into something he shouldn't be." She hesitated. "Lately he's been acting strange. Keeping to himself a lot."

I expected her to say more. When she didn't I said, "Susan, I can't help Petey if you don't level with me."

Her eyes widened and when I followed her gaze I saw Petey walking toward us. He was big for an eighth grader. Almost five-nine with a slim, athletic body. He wore a Nike sweatshirt and torn jeans.

He tugged on his Red Sox cap. "My sister and my teacher. Wow. Are you two on a date or something?"

Susan smiled. "Actually we're talking about you."

Petey's eyes stayed focused on me as if Susan hadn't spoken.

"Sit down," I said. "I'll buy you a Coke."

"Nah. I gotta get home. Got a big history project due tomorrow." He grinned. "If I buy you a Coke will I get a better grade?"

I laughed.

"Didn't think so," he said.

"Susan and I were trying to figure out why you're getting into so much trouble lately. Is something bothering you?"

He shrugged. "Guess I have a lot of stuff on my mind."

"Talk to me, Petey," I said.

He hesitated and I could tell from his expression there was something more he wanted to say. Then he sighed. "Mom told me Susan was here. She's not feeling well. Wants her home."

"You can speak directly to me, Petey," Susan said.

"Yeah. Sure." He walked toward the door.

Susan slid across the booth and got up. "Sorry. Maybe we can do this another time."

I nodded. "Call me anytime you want to talk."

Susan leaned close to my ear. "Petey's a good kid, but someday he's going to get into more trouble than he can handle. We've both got to help him."

Then she turned and left.

CHAPTER 1

TWO WEEKS LATER

The phone rang at two o'clock in the morning. For a split second I wasn't sure where I was. It rang again. My mind flashed to my mother's face. Something must have happened.

I swung my legs to the floor, reached for the receiver and cradled it against my ear. "Hello," I said.

There was a long pause. Then a voice said, "Mr. Asher?" It was young and tentative. Just a kid.

I let out a breath and my shoulders relaxed. "If this is one of my students asking how to do a homework assignment I'm going to be really upset."

Another pause. I flipped on the lamp beside the bed. Beth nudged me with her elbow, then leaned against the headboard and pushed the hair out of her eyes. I winked.

"It's Petey Oliver, Mr. Asher."

I sat up straighter. "Are you all right?"

"Yeah, I'm okay." He hesitated. "Remember when you told me if I ever needed to talk to someone I could come to you?"

"I remember. Where are you?"

"You gotta promise you won't tell," he said.

"Petey, the police have been searching for you for three days. Your mother's frantic. Where the hell are you?"

He was silent for so long I thought he had hung up. I heard a sharp intake of breath as if he was smoking a cigarette. "Tell me where you are," I said. "I'll come and get you. We'll talk."

"I found something," he said.

"What?"

"I don't know what it means. I just...just want to talk about it."

"Okay."

"Shit. I hear noises." His voice was lower, almost a hiss. "I think someone's coming."

"Petey, dial nine-one-one right now. Tell them where you are and hide until they get there."

"I'll be at Walden Pond," he said softly. "In front of the bath house. If you bring anyone I'm splitting. No one will ever see me again." He hung up.

I turned to Beth. We had spent part of last night talking about Petey. "He wants me to meet him at Walden," I said. "He found something and wants to talk about it."

"Is he okay?"

I got up and began to pull on my jeans. "I don't know. He sounded scared."

"I'll come with you."

"He'll take off if I bring anyone."

"I'll wait in the car. You talk to him. Then we can both take him home."

Damn it, I wanted to say. You're doing it again. Instead I just shook my head.

She closed her eyes for a few seconds. We'd recently gotten back together after a six-year separation. This wasn't the way I hoped this night would turn out.

I sat on the bed and put my hand on her shoulder. "Look, I'm sorry. Why don't you stay until I get back. You can look after Richard. Maybe take him for a walk or read the morning paper to him."

"Taking care of your parakeet is not what I had in mind for this morning." She watched me dress for a minute then climbed out of bed. "I got some things to do today anyway." She started to put on her clothes.

"Beth, you know how important you are to me. I want our relationship to work this time, but I have to do this."

She nodded, but I could tell from her expression that she was upset.

I went into the bathroom and splashed water on my face. When I came back into the bedroom Beth was dressed. "I'll call you when I'm through," I said.

"Tell Petey I hope everything's all right." She kissed me lightly on the lips and walked out the door.

I grabbed my windbreaker, flipped off the lights and sprinted to my T-Bird. The November air felt raw against my skin.

Beth's car was rounding the turn at the end of the street. Six years ago she'd complained that I spent too much time with my students. This was different. Surely, she was able to see that.

My mind switched to Petey as I drove. He was bright, rebellious and needy. Three days ago after arguing with a teacher he had walked out of school. No one had seen him since.

The police, neighbors, Petey's mother and two older sisters had spent the last few days searching. I had done some looking on my own. The problem was he had run away three times before and eventually came back. Most people thought it would happen again.

Petey spent a lot of afternoons in my classroom when he wasn't serving detention. He was different from most of my students. More independent and funny in a mature way. He had a lot of friends, but at times I felt he'd rather spend his time with adults than hang out with kids his own age, and when he finished his school work he was always reading as if he couldn't learn enough. He was the kind of kid who thought he knew all the answers. The problem was, he was still only thirteen.

There wasn't a car on the road this time of the morning. Petey's words echoed in my mind and I wondered if what he found had made him run away. Then I thought of the fear in his voice when he heard someone coming. I stepped hard on the gas.

Fifteen minutes later I arrived at Walden. A half moon glistened off the surface of the pond just visible at the bottom of a steep embankment.

I nosed my car off the street. In the distance I could see the roof of the bathhouse.

I popped open the glove compartment, took out a flashlight and tested the beam. The batteries appeared strong.

A wooden gate with "No Parking" stenciled across it was closed and blocked the walkway which led to the water. I moved onto the grass and went around it.

The black-topped surface of the path was cracked and overgrown with crabgrass. Fallen leaves blew across it. Rows of maples and pine lined both sides, their interlocking branches forming a tunnel. A gusty wind whistled off the pond. The air smelled sweet from the trees.

I flashed my light up ahead. The bath house was a few hundred feet away. A flagstone walkway was in front of it and cement steps led to a sandy beach area on the right. I walked slowly and aimed my light toward the building. "Petey," I yelled.

No response.

The wind picked up and the trees around me trembled. The sky was clear, the moon clearly visible. Stars shone through the branches of the trees.

I pointed the light toward a path which circled the perimeter of the water. I had walked the two mile trail many times. In the darkness it looked different, almost spooky.

"Petey," I yelled again. "It's Mr. Asher." I hesitated waiting for an answer." "Don't play games. I'm not in the mood."

I flashed my light toward the building and began to inch closer. Trees were clustered behind it. Big ones with thick trunks rising against the blackness of the night sky. Their branches were knocking together in the wind.

A door marked 'first aid' was closed and locked. Despite the cold I could feel my sweater starting to stick to my body. I silently cursed my decision not to call the police.

I circled around the right side of the building and pointed my light up the hill. Steps led to the street. I climbed a few and focused my light on a gravel walkway. There was no one around.

I felt my stomach tighten. Be calm, I said to myself. Relax. Petey's fine. He's just waiting to make sure you're alone. He probably just climbed the hill up to the road to check for cops. I'll give him ten minutes. If he doesn't show by then I'll do what I should have done in the first place.

I walked down the steps to the water's edge and waved my light around. If Petey was here I wanted to make sure he could see me.

I leaned against the lifeguard's chair and looked out at the water. I thought about last spring when I had taken fifty-five eighth graders to visit the site of Thoreau's cabin. I had talked to them for about twenty minutes when a student asked if Thoreau had gone to the bathroom in the pond. They all groaned. Several looked toward the water yelling, "gross". Then they wanted to know what time we were going to Burger King.

I turned back to the bathhouse and looked at my watch. Fifteen minutes had passed, but I was reluctant to leave. My instincts told me he would come.

I walked slowly back toward the cement walkway. The wind had died down and the stillness made me feel uneasy.

Then I heard a sharp crack in the distance as if a tree limb had been broken. It seemed to come from a curve in the pond to my right, but in the darkness it was hard to tell. Then branches crackled. The noise seemed closer to me.

I flashed my light toward the path. It reflected off a cement wall.

Something moaned. It was low, almost a growl. Hard to tell if it was even human. Then I heard a splash and more rustling of the trees, this time moving away from me.

My gut told me to leave, but I couldn't. I had to find out what had made those noises. Petey might be in trouble.

I kept the light leveled in front of me and began to jog down a narrow path near the water. I reached a boat launch and stopped. "Petey," I yelled. My flash focused on a sign that said 'Danger Unguarded'. You're getting too old for this shit, I said to myself.

On the other side of the launch the trail was wider. It inclined and curved slightly. I stepped over tree roots and tried to avoid the large rocks. A small wire fence on my right ripped my jacket. I stopped, took a deep breath and listened. Silence. I moved slowly ahead and flashed the light around. The beam reflected off the trees. Nothing was moving. Maybe I had heard an animal.

I continued slowly along the path. It curved more to the right and the slope down to the water got steeper. I aimed the light at the pond, then moved it along the shoreline. I could feel sweat rolling down my back.

I was about to go back toward the bathhouse when something caught my eye. I flashed my light in front of me, angling it toward the water. At first I thought it might be just a large boulder in the water. Then I saw the arms stretched out in front.

"Oh God. No."

I ran ahead. The wire fence had been knocked over and I jumped down the slope. The body was face down and only a few feet from shore. I pointed my light at it. Gummy strands of blood floated around it. My stomach flipped violently. Then I saw her long blonde hair.

I threw the light on the sand, waded into the water, gripped her legs and pulled. Her dress slid up to her waist. I dragged her onto a patch of grass, grabbed her shoulders and gave a twist. She turned face up. "Jesus," I said. My stomach flipped again.

The side of her head was caved in. Blood dribbled onto the sand and her body appeared bloated. Her eyes were sunken and lips swollen. Bile entered my mouth and for an instant I thought I was going to throw up. I closed my eyes for a few seconds. Then I refocused on the body.

I studied her face. Any thoughts of saving her were gone. I shut my eyes and turned away. When I looked back I realized who the dead woman was. It was Susan Oliver, Petey's sister.

CHAPTER 2

I took one more look at Susan. Her skirt was bunched up around her waist. I pulled it down, then picked up the light and flashed it around. Whoever had done this was still close by. They could be watching me. I climbed back to the path and began to run. The beam bobbed and weaved in front of me.

Where the hell was Petey? Maybe he saw what happened and took off. He had told me he and Susan were always fighting. I didn't think he was capable of doing this, but right now I wasn't sure.

There was a pay phone across from the pond. I fumbled putting the quarter into the slot and dialed nine-one-one. "Susan Oliver," I said. "I found her body at Walden. She's dead. I'm there now." I stared toward the water, trying to catch my breath.

"Could you state your name, sir?" the dispatcher said.

I told her. She made me repeat what I had found.

"An ambulance will be right there," she said. "Stay close to the phone. They'll find you."

I walked across the street, got into my car, locked the doors and stared into the trees. My instincts told me to search for Petey and make sure he was all right, but my mind kept picturing the blood in the water and Susan's body. I'd wait for the cops.

A few minutes later I saw flashing lights. The ambulance pulled off the roadway, nosing close to the closed wooden gate. Two paramedics hopped out.

I got out of the car and moved toward them. "Down there," I said pointing. "About a quarter mile along the path to the left. I found her face down in the water. She's dead."

They grabbed a backboard and a black satchel. One of them snapped on a flashlight. "Show us," he said.

We raced down the black-topped walkway and onto the path. The clomping of our footsteps was the only sound. I flashed my light toward the body, then waited as they went down the slope.

They crouched over the body. Neither said a word. I turned away.

Within seconds I saw another beam of light, then heard footsteps. Two patrolmen came up the path. One jumped down the slope. The other stayed with me.

He watched the paramedics for a few seconds, then turned. "Are you okay?" he said.

"There's a kid around here," I said. "Petey Oliver. He..."

The officer held up his hand. "The Petey Oliver that everyone's looking for?"

I nodded. "That's his sister, Susan. He called and told me to meet him here. We've got to start looking."

The officer stared at me and was about to respond when two other officers arrived. The three of them huddled for a few minutes. I pointed my light into the trees and moved it around.

The two officers went down the slope. The other turned to me. "Everything's going to be taken care of," he said. "Must have been a hell of a shock. You sure you're all right?"

I nodded.

"Why don't you come with me." He started to move up the path.

"You don't understand," I said. "If Petey sees all of you, he's going to run away. If he sees me, he'll stay. I can talk to him."

The officer continued along the path.

I put my hand on his shoulder. "We're wasting time," I said.

He stopped, turned slowly and looked at my hand. I let it drop.

"Lieutenant Nash is on his way. He'll want to talk to you."

We walked up to the street. I'd wait for Nash. Maybe he'd understand.

The officer opened the back door of the cruiser. "You can wait here," he said.

I climbed in and rested my head on the seat. The officer gripped the door, stared at me for a few seconds, then leaned against the fender.

I studied the pond. The police radio stuttered a deadpan murmur followed by an interval of static. I could feel my frustration growing.

Minutes later an unmarked car pulled up. The man who got out pushed his fingers through his gray hair. His tie hung loose around his neck. For a second our eyes locked, then he approached the officer. He was well over six feet and towered over the patrolman as they talked. He turned, pointed his light down the path and began to walk.

I jumped out of the cruiser. "Lieutenant Nash," I said.

The man stopped and turned toward me. "You knew the woman." He said it as a fact not a question. He turned to the patrolman, whispered for a few seconds, then continued down the path.

"Lieutenant," I yelled. "Petey Oliver is somewhere around here."

"I know," he said without breaking stride.

The officer motioned with his head for me to get back inside. I climbed in. This time he closed the door. I drummed my fingers on my knee. Thoreau had said, "The savage man is never quite eradicated." For the first time I felt I really understood.

I shook my head and stared toward the pond. Jesus, I had just seen Susan two weeks ago. I went over the conversation we had at the coffee shop in my mind and remembered the tension I felt between Petey and Susan. So how had she ended up here?

Another cruiser pulled up. Two state police officers talked to the patrolman, then headed down the path.

It was at least an hour before Lieutenant Nash made his way up the walkway and approached the cruiser. He opened the door and I climbed out.

He had a white handkerchief in his hand and he was rubbing his nose. "Allergies," he said. "Drive me crazy. You ever had allergies?"

I shook my head. "Any sign of Petey?"

"My men are looking."

"Lieutenant, if Petey sees all the cops he'll run off. He may not if he sees me."

"If the kid's around, we'll find him." He pulled a note pad out of his pocket. "Shame," he said. "A young woman like that. Some guys say they get used to it. I'd rather work with the ones that don't." He shook his head. "Any idea how old she is?"

"Susan's twenty-eight," I said.

Laughter came from the direction of the pond. The lieutenant looked toward the sound for a few seconds, then refocused on me.

"Your name's Asher?"

I nodded.

"Mr. Asher, why don't you tell me what happened."

I told him about Petey's phone call and how I found Susan's body. He shook his head. "Phone calls in the middle of the night are always a bitch. Drive my wife crazy. Bet your wife was annoyed."

"I'm not married," I said.

He held up his hand, turned his head and sneezed loudly into his handkerchief. When he turned back he was wiping his nose. "Sorry," he said. "How well did you know Susan?"

"I met her once to talk about Petey."

"Anything social?"

"Not really," I said.

He smiled. "Is that a yes or a no?"

"We had coffee together once. She was concerned that Petey was getting into trouble at school. Wanted to know what she could do."

The wind started to gust and leaves blew across the sidewalk. I zipped up my jacket.

Nash wrote something on his pad. "You knew how old she was?"

"She told me."

"How'd Petey feel about his sister?"

I shrugged. "Didn't talk about her that much. Told me once they didn't get along, but who knows."

Nash pointed to the rip in my jacket. "How'd that happen?"

"I tore it on the wire fence."

He fingered the hole then said, "You think the kid would be capable of doing this to his sister?"

I shook my head.

Nash looked away. When he turned back I couldn't read his expression. "If Petey was around and saw what happened, he could be in shock. Young kid like that. It'd take him a while to get over it. I've seen it happen too many times. Kids just freak. Won't talk. Won't eat. I hope for his sake he didn't see it." He ran his hand through his hair and stared at me.

"That's why we have to find him," I said.

He nodded. "I know. Anything you can tell me about the kid that'll help."

"He's street smart. Knows his way around. Petey's a thinker and a worrier. He's got a vivid imagination too."

"How'd he sound on the phone?"

"Scared and confused. Told me he found something. Didn't say what it was, but he wanted to talk about it?"

"Would have been better if you called us right off, you know?"

"I know," I said. "But at the time I felt I didn't have a choice."

Footsteps thudded on the walkway behind us. A cop waved to Nash then flashed his light toward the parking lot across the street. He crossed and disappeared into the darkness.

The palms of my hands were clammy and I wiped them against my jacket.

"Teaching must be a tough job," Nash said. "Thoreau was a teacher for awhile." He hesitated. "Many students call you at home?"

"I've been teaching for twelve years. Sometimes a student really gets to you and you want to help anyway you can. I gave Petey my number and told him if he ever needed to talk he could call. I don't do that with many students."

"You feel up to going to the station and making a statement?"

"Yeah," I said.

I shoved my hands in my jacket pockets. My greatest fear remained unspoken. What if whoever killed Susan had taken Petey. What if Petey were dead. I looked up the road in the direction of the dump. "You gonna look there?" I said.

"We're going to look everywhere, Mr. Asher." He pointed toward my neck. "Would you unbutton your shirt, please, sir."

"Excuse me."

"Unbutton your shirt."

I pulled down my sweater and unbuttoned the top three buttons.

Nash took a penlight out of his pocket and flashed it at my neck. He tugged on my shirt collar, squinted and moved closer. "Do you ever wear any type of medal around your neck?"

"Sometimes," I said.

He flipped off the light. "How about a black onyx medallion about the size of a quarter?"

I shook my head. "Why?"

"You know anyone who wears one like that?" he said.

"Petey wears a medallion like that," I said.

CHAPTER 3

After signing a statement at the police station, I headed toward home. I had spent most of the last two hours waiting and thinking. I couldn't get the image of Susan's face out of my mind.

As I drove by Sacred Heart Church I pulled into the lot, then went inside and sat in a pew. I looked at the stained glass windows and smelled the incense. I've always liked churches and Sacred Heart was where my family went every Sunday when I was a kid. It felt good to sit in the quiet and think. I sat for about ten minutes, then lit a couple of candles. I said a prayer for Susan. Then one for Petey. I slipped a twenty into the donation box as I left.

When I finally pulled into my driveway it was after seven and I could hardly keep my head up. I wanted to call Beth and let her know what happened, but I felt drained. I sat in the car, closed my eyes and leaned back in the seat.

I had lived on the top floor of a two-family house for the past six years, ever since my divorce. My landlord, Dave Paulini, had advertised for a middle-aged, quiet, professional person. I figured one out of three wasn't bad.

Dave was a widower, in his mid-eighties, and lived on the bottom floor. I was glad that he was spending the night with his sister. He was an early riser. If he heard me coming in he'd want to talk. I did-n't feel like talking about Susan yet.

I got out of the car and slowly walked up the stairs to the front door. Luckily it was Saturday. All I wanted to do was sleep.

I walked into the hallway. The door to my apartment was on the right. The first thing I noticed was that it was open a few inches. Then I saw the splintered door frame. "Shit," I said. "Not again." This was the third time my apartment had been broken into over the past six months.

I pushed the door open a few more inches and listened. Silence. Stairs from the hallway led directly into my kitchen. I slowly walked up. Two chairs were toppled. Broken fragments of dishes and glasses were scattered on the floor. Drawers had been pulled out and emptied. I rushed over to Richard. In the chaos of the kitchen his cage stood undisturbed.

"Must have been done by a bird lover," I mumbled. Richard cooed softly and cocked his head. "You're supposed to stop people from doing this," I said. "You couldn't have pecked out nine-one-one?"

The living room was in similar shape. Two book cases had been emptied, my books and compact discs lay on the floor. The cushions of my overstuffed couch looked as if someone had flung them across the room and my glass coffee table was on its side. I picked the phone off the floor and dialed nine-one-one for the second time today. The dispatcher said an officer would be over.

I walked through the rest of the apartment. Each room had been ransacked, but this break-in was different from the others. Nothing seemed to be missing. Even the small sum of cash I kept in my bureau drawer had been thrown on the floor. It was the viciousness that bothered me. I thought about the phone call that got me out of the apartment and my discovery of Susan. There had to be a connection.

I went back into the living room. I wanted to pick up my compact discs and stack them on the shelf just to be doing something, but I couldn't touch anything until the cops arrived. The last time someone broke in they had taken half my collection. I had pictured the person going through my discs to decide which ones were good enough to steal.

Richard whistled as I waited. "Don't try and make up," I said. "You should have made me get that alarm system. Problem is, if I buy it, I might not have enough money to live here so I'd have to move. Maybe I should start charging you rent."

I looked at the debris still lying on the floor and shook my head. I was glad Beth had decided to go back to her place. I was lost in thought when there was a knock on the door.

Officer Rita Dooley was the first to enter. "This is beginning to be a habit," she said. "Maybe we should keep someone on this street to handle your break-ins full time."

I smiled. "I think I'm going to start leaving the door open and put out a welcome mat. It'll save me from getting the locks fixed."

Rita and I had worked together at school on a program to help gang members make better decisions. We had dated a couple of times before I got back with Beth. It felt good to see a familiar face. The second officer I didn't know.

Rita looked at the kitchen. "Jesus," she said shaking her head. Then she motioned toward her partner. "Steve, this is Frank Hollowell."

Hollowell was around fifty. His face was round and jowly and his hair was pushed to one side covering a bald spot. He nodded and walked into the living room.

"What'd they take this time?" Rita said.

"Nothing."

She looked toward the living room. "Can't say as I blame them."

Rita was in her mid-thirties. Short red hair and freckles. She looked as Irish as her name. She took out a note pad and turned to me. Hollowell headed toward the bedroom.

"What time did it happen?"

"Sometime between two-thirty and seven this morning."

"Anyone know you weren't going to be home?"

I shook my head and told her about Petey Oliver's phone call and how I had found Susan's body. I could feel my voice breaking as I talked.

"I heard about Susan's death," Rita said. "I didn't know you found her. Are you okay?"

I shrugged. Then I told her my suspicions about the phone call.

Rita stared at her note pad for several seconds. "Petey could have been calling from anywhere. You think he might have wanted to get you out of your apartment?"

"I don't know. The phone call and break-in seem like too much of a coincidence. Whoever broke in was looking for something specific. I can't figure out what or how it might be connected to Susan's murder. It couldn't have been Petey. The cops found his medallion at Walden." I shook my head. "Am I making sense?"

"Yeah and I think you might be right about the connection."

She asked me a few more questions, then closed her note pad.

Hollowell came back into the kitchen just as she finished.

"You got any enemies, Asher?" he said.

"Just students who think I give them too much homework."

He didn't smile.

"Nothing's missing," Rita said to Hollowell. She turned to me. "We'll get someone to dust the place. Then we'll check with the neighbors to see if they saw anything. Is there somewhere you can go for a couple of hours?"

"I got a key to Dave's place. I'll hang around there. Maybe get some sleep. Dave should be home soon."

Rita nodded.

I walked out to the sidewalk and took a deep breath to try and clear my head. The neighborhood was quiet. Yesterday was trash day and several plastic barrels were on the sidewalk. The houses were all two family. Each one built up against the next with small plots of land in the back and hedges up against the building. Most of the families had lived here for years. I could live in this neighborhood for twenty years and still be the "new guy".

I was stretched out on Dave's couch, sound asleep, when I felt a hand shake my shoulder. It was Dave.

"What's happened," he said. "What's a cruiser doing out front. Not another break-in?"

I rubbed my hands across my eyes and sat up. "Yeah." Funny thing is they didn't take anything. Just messed my apartment up a little."

"Are you all right?"

I nodded. "I wasn't home."

Dave shook his head. "This was always a safe neighborhood. We gotta do something about this. I wish I was here. I could have stopped it."

"If you were here you could have gotten hurt. I'm glad you picked tonight to stay with your sister."

Dave blushed. "I wasn't at my sister's. I spent the night with Mildred."

Mildred Pearson had been Dave's girlfriend for the past two months. She was the first woman Dave had dated since the death of his wife twelve years ago. He was concerned that she was too young for him. Dave is eighty-four. Mildred is seventy-five.

I smiled. "You probably didn't get much sleep last night, either."
Dave blushed again.

"I hope you two are practicing safe sex."

Dave tilted his head. "And where did you spend the night? Don't tell me you finally got a woman to go out with you."

"Actually I was with Beth until I got the phone call." I told him about what had happened.

Dave put his hand on my shoulder. "That poor Mrs. Oliver," he said. "How much can one woman take. This is the second one of her children to die."

"Second one?" I said.

He nodded. "You didn't know? Happened about five years ago. Must have been the summer you were in California. Kid was sixteen. Drowned in the Connecticut River."

"Petey never mentioned an older brother to me."

"Dwight was his name. He went to live with his father when the family split up six years ago."

I was about to respond when there was a knock on the door. It was Rita. Hollowell stood behind her.

"Steve, we're through upstairs," she said. "Didn't find much of anything. None of the neighbors saw anything suspicious. You gonna be all right?"

"Nothing six days of sleep won't help."

She grinned. "You're pretty calm about these break-ins"

"It's one of my character flaws. I try to remain reasonable at all times."

"This one's different," she said. "It's not normal to smash a place up like that."

I shrugged. "Probably just kids."

"Maybe someone thinks you saw something at Walden."

"So they came over and thrashed my apartment. I don't think so."

"All I'm saying is be careful. We could put a cruiser outside for awhile."

I shook my head. "I think you're overreacting."

"You might want to buy an alarm system," Rita said.

I nodded. "Richard and I have discussed it. Do me a favor? If you hear anything about Petey, call me?"

Our eyes locked for a few seconds and I could tell by her expression she felt Petey was in danger. She probably thought I was in danger too.

She nodded. "If you need to talk, call me at home."

Hollowell chuckled. "You two know each other, do you?"

"Can it, Hollowell," Rita said as she closed the door.

"You wanna sleep on the couch till I get the locks fixed," Dave said.

I shook my head.

"What if whoever broke in decides to come back."

"I don't think they would. Especially during the daylight. Whatever they were looking for they either found it or they know I don't have it. They'd have no reason to come back."

Dave and I talked for a few more minutes. When I left I double-locked the door in the hallway. Then I slowly walked up the stairs. I couldn't face cleaning up the mess. I sat on the couch and thought about what Nash had said about Petey. If he had seen what happened he could be in shock.

My mind flashed back to when my father died. I was eleven. He had gone into the hospital complaining of indigestion. They kept him overnight as a precaution. During the night an aneurysm burst and he died.

I remembered my mother's face when she woke me. It was white and her eyes were bloodshot.

"Dad's died," she said quietly. Then she put her arms around me.

At first I didn't understand. All I could do was nod. It didn't quite register.

We hugged for a while, then Mom went into her bedroom to lie down. I got up, drank some juice and went out into the yard, not really sad, just trying to imagine what it was like being dead. I sat with my back against an oak tree, staring up into the sunlight. When I closed my eyes Dad was there, smiling like he always did, asking if I wanted to throw a football around. Then I realized I was day-dreaming. It was the first time I remember crying as a kid.

I wondered how Mrs. Oliver was coping with her pain.

I called Beth and told her about finding Susan's body. I rambled a lot trying to sort things out in my mind. Then I told her about the break-in and what I said to the cops. "I can't get the vision of Susan out of my mind and I'm worried about Petey. What if whoever killed Susan has him. What if he's already dead?"

"You want to come over?"

"It's tempting, but what I need now is sleep. Maybe it'll clear my head."

"It might do you good to be with someone."

"Not now. Maybe later. What really pisses me off is that cop suspects me."

"That's ridiculous."

"Not to them. Hell, when I was telling Nash about going to Walden to meet Petey and stumbling over Susan's body I almost didn't believe it myself. Just seemed like too much of a coincidence, like someone was setting me up."

"Petey?"

"I don't know."

Beth was silent for several seconds, then she said, "I've got to go to Rockport tonight. Some of my paintings are being shown in a gallery. I already made the commitment, but if you want me to cancel I will."

"No. You go ahead. I'll see you when you get back."

"You wanna come. We can stay at an inn. Come back tomorrow night?"

"Right now all I want to do is sleep," I said. "If I change my mind I'll call you."

"Okay. "I won't be back until late Sunday. I'll call you."

We talked for a few more minutes. Then I hung up.

I felt better after talking to Beth. She usually had that effect on me. We had been divorced for six years, but had started to date six months ago after running into each other in Hyannis on the Cape. At first we'd had dinner, gone to a couple of movies and spent the night together a few times. We both wanted to take it slow. Lately we'd seen each other almost every night. The feelings that I had for her six years ago had returned. I wanted her to move in with me, but I could tell by some of the conversations we'd had she wasn't ready. Ordinarily I'd jump at the chance to spend the weekend with her at an inn. Today I didn't feel up to it and my state of mind wouldn't help any doubts Beth might be having about our relationship.

I leaned the bookcases against the wall, then picked up some discs and began to alphabetize them on the shelf. I was torn between wanting the phone to ring and not wanting it to. I was afraid of what news I might hear about Petey.

I finished straightening the living room, then settled back on the couch to get some sleep. It was when I started to doze that I realized what was missing.

CHAPTER 4

My video cassettes, all six tapes, were gone. I own a copy of "The Treasure of Sierra Madre" and a few Woody Allen movies. Those, as well as, a blank cassette I've used so many times for taping shows from television it was wearing thin, were missing.

It didn't make sense. Why would someone leave my television and stereo, even my money, but take my cassettes and then ransack the place as if looking for more?

It had to have something to do with Susan's death. The timing was too much of a coincidence. Whoever broke in must have thought I had concealed something on the videos, and that they were important enough to steal. As I dozed off, I ran through Petey's phone conversation one more time.

The sound of a car engine and voices outside woke me at four in the afternoon. I looked out the window. A van from a Boston television station was parked on the street. A woman with a video camera was taking pictures of the house, and a few other people stood on the sidewalk sipping coffee. Dave was talking to a woman who was jotting things in a notebook. The media were the last people I felt like talking to.

My back ached from sleeping on the couch. I stretched, then called the cops to report the missing cassettes. Rita Dooley wasn't at the station. The officer who answered said there was no news on Petey.

I had a sudden urge to be with Beth. To see her face and hear her laugh. Maybe what I needed was a couple of days away with her. I dialed her number. When her machine picked up, I left a message for her to call me.

I did a few knee bends, then jogged in place for a few minutes. When I finished I dug my guitar out of the closet, sat on the couch and played a few chords. I had played in a rock band in high school and paid my way through college doing gigs at local clubs. I wrote all the band's music. Pete Townshend was my hero and everything I wrote seemed to sound like The Who songs. I strummed the chords to "Won't get Fooled Again." Usually playing guitar relaxed me. Not today.

I straightened out the bedroom and took a shower. I let hot water run over my body and scrubbed my skin roughly. I was reluctant to get out. I had just finished dressing when there was a knock on the door.

"Steve. It's Dave."

He had on a blue blazer, gray pants and a white shirt. Saturday night was when he took Mildred dancing at the Italian-American club. He let out a low whistle as he entered the kitchen. "This is terrible," he said waving his hand at the mess.

I shrugged. "I kind of like the look. I was thinking of keeping it this way."

"Nothing was taken?" he said.

"My video collection's missing. Maybe they were upset I didn't have a copy of 'Casablanca' so they trashed the place."

Dave shook his head. "Why would someone want your videos?"

"Obviously it was someone with good taste," I said. "I saw you talking to the press. You a celebrity now?"

He grinned. "I had to head them off. Figured you didn't want to talk to them. Told them you had gone away for a few days. Most of them left, but a couple are still out there."

"Thanks. The reporters have anything useful to say?"

"That nice lady from Channel Four told me the cops have picked up Susan's ex-husband for questioning."

"I didn't know she had been married."

He nodded. "Got married when she was twenty. Only lasted six months. She had a restraining order against him."

I shook my head. As terrible as Susan's death was, I hoped her ex-husband was the killer and the police could prove it.

"They say anything else?"

He hesitated, looked at Richard's cage, then refocused on me. "Guy from The Herald said a cop told him off the record that you were one of the top suspects."

"Shit. They're not going to print that, are they?"

"Probably not after all the lies I told them about what a wonderful guy you are. I made you sound like Saint Steve."

"The School Committee reads I'm a suspect and they may think I'm not fit to be in the classroom. It would be just like them to suspend me until the investigation is over."

"What about your students? How would they handle the news?"

All sorts of thoughts whizzed through my mind. It was one thing to think Nash was questioning me like I was a suspect, but another to have the cops actually say it.

"Steve?"

I smiled and tried to keep the anger out of my voice. "They'd probably think it was cool."

"I just cooked up a pound of spaghetti," Dave said. "You want some?"

"Sure. Can I bring Richard? He loves your spaghetti."

"Only if he wears a tux."

One of Dave's hobbies was cooking. Another seemed to be feeding me, which I didn't mind at all. I had gained fifteen pounds since I had moved into my apartment. If I didn't play basketball at least three times a week, by this time next year I'd weigh over two hundred pounds.

I looked at my watch. It was seven p.m. Beth must have already headed out to Rockport.

"Give me ten minutes," I said.

When Dave left I got out my address book and dialed Lisa Gerrault, a lawyer friend of mine. I wanted some advice on what to do if the cops started to question me. Her machine picked up and I left a message.

I sat for a few minutes longer. As a teacher, my reputation was important to me. Any hint of a scandal could destroy that. I always like to be in control and pride myself on being able to handle tough situations.

My mind drifted back almost twenty years. I was a sophomore at Northeastern University in Boston. Mitch Wheeler was my roommate. As the year progressed I noticed changes in his behavior. He became quiet and started to cut classes. When I realized he had a drug problem I tried to help him. One night I came home and he was stoned. We stayed up and talked about what he was doing to himself and how drugs could ruin his life. It didn't work. Two days later he died of a Cocaine overdose.

The horror of Mitch's death and the guilt I felt about not doing enough to help him turned to fear when the police conducted an investigation. Rumors circulated, as stories always did among college students during the seventies. The most damaging was that our dorm room had been a center for dealing drugs. The stories weren't true, but the cop who questioned me seemed to believe them. He confronted me on my drug use, and although I smoked an occasional joint, I denied ever using drugs.

From the cops demeanor I expected to be charged with drug possession and my teaching career would be over before it even started. No charges were ever filed, but when I graduated and got my first teaching job I still had a fear that those stories were in a police file somewhere and someday they'd materialize and I'd be forced to stop teaching because of the revelations. I remembered another teacher who, a few years ago, had been accused of using drugs during the sixties. The allegations caused so much controversy that he was forced to resign.

As tragic as Susan's murder was I wasn't about to let my name be drawn into the investigation if I could help it.

I spent the next thirty minutes at Dave's dining room table demolishing two plates of pasta, half a loaf of fresh baked garlic bread and a glass of homemade wine. He didn't eat. Told me he couldn't dance on a full stomach. He had made all of this food for me.

We talked about the Celtics, the Patriots and the Red Sox. Dave once again told me that garlic, which he put into everything, was a key ingredient to a longer life. With all the garlic he used, if he was right, he'd live to be two hundred. At times I had trouble concentrating on what we were talking about.

I went back upstairs. I didn't have the energy to tackle the mess in the kitchen yet so I plopped on the couch. Petey's phone call puzzled me. He must have called Susan, too. Why else would she have been at Walden? Unless she had gone there first and Petey had followed her. But why wouldn't he have mentioned it to me on the phone? And where did Susan's ex-husband fit into all of this? I hate to admit it when I'm confused. I tried to teach my students how to think logically, and it bothered me that I couldn't even put what had happened into some type of chronological order.

"Where the hell are you, Petey?" I muttered aloud.

I needed some answers. I put on my jacket and headed out to my car. The night was cold even for November. There was a feel of snow in the air. There were no members of the press to block my way.

The Olivers lived about two miles away, on the other side of the city. I wanted to see if there was anything I could do for the family, but I also felt a need to talk to Susan's mother. Maybe she knew what Susan had been doing last night.

Streetlights had been installed on the common behind City Hall. A few homeless people with blankets wrapped around them were camped out on the grass. Waltham had two homeless shelters, but there never seemed to be enough beds.

The Olivers lived in one of the city's poorer neighborhoods. The Irish had first lived here, then Italians. Now it was a mixed neighborhood with a variety of ethnic groups. The houses were packed together. Many were crumbling from neglect. New owners had been buying up places around here and fixing them up. They hadn't reached the Olivers' neighborhood yet.

Their house was a run-down one-story ranch that looked like it hadn't been painted since it was built. A small patch of what had once been lawn lined the front. From the outside the house appeared small. Six people had once lived in it. I wondered how they all fit.

The outside porch light was on as if they were expecting someone, and I could see the blue glow of a television set as I walked up the front steps and rang the bell.

The door opened slightly, kept in place by a chain lock. "Yes," a female voice said.

"I'm Steve Asher, Petey's teacher," I said. "I was wondering if I could talk to Mrs. Oliver?"

"Just a minute," she said.

The door closed for several seconds, then opened wider. The woman stepped out on the front steps, buttoned her coat and pulled the door shut behind her. She was in her early twenties. Her hair was dark, short and spiked. A large hoop-earring dangled from one ear. She looked like Susan, but her features were harder, not as pretty. "My mother's not up to seeing anyone."

"I'm sorry about your sister," I said.

She pulled her coat collar up. "You talked to Petey. How come you didn't call the cops and tell them where he was? They would have gotten him. Maybe Susan would still be alive."

"Believe me, if I had it to do over again I would."

She lowered her head and closed her eyes for a few seconds. Petey had mentioned an older sister, Cynthia. He told me she lived in New York City and seldom came home, even for holidays. He had only talked to her once in the past two years. "She's an actress," he told me. "Someday she's gonna be famous."

I hoped she was better at acting than at being a sister.

She refocused on me. "If something's happened to him, my mother won't be able to handle it." She spoke so quietly I almost couldn't hear her.

"It might do your mother good to talk about what happened."

"My mother's sleeping," she said. Then she clenched her fist and her eyes narrowed. "You fuckin' do-gooders. You think you can solve everything with just the right words." Her voice rose. "Well, fuck you. What'd you do, sit around your fancy house, snap your fingers, and say 'Hey I got an idea. I'll go visit the Olivers. Show them I'm concerned.' You never gave a shit about Petey. You don't even know him. Kid's evil. I warned Susan not to trust him. She wouldn't listen."

I felt my anger starting to rise and had to stop myself from shouting back at her. I could only imagine the pain she was going through.

"I don't think Petey could have done this," I said trying to keep the irritation out of my voice.

She drummed her fingers along the porch railing. Two people standing on a porch across the street watched us. When they saw me look over they went inside the house.

"Petey said he found something," I said. "Any idea what it might be?"

"Found something? Is that what he told you? He stole it. We already told the police. Kid's always been a crook."

"What'd he take?"

"Money. All we had. It wasn't much, but at least we pay the rent and put food on the table. Now what are we supposed to do? How do we pay for Susan's funeral? Petey doesn't give a shit about us. He's probably far away from here by now."

"I don't think so. He wouldn't have asked to meet me."

"Kid's a con man, Mr. Teacher. He enjoys all this attention. He was just messing with you, trying to make a fool out of you." She shook her head and sighed. "It sure worked."

"Did Petey call the house last night?"

"Who knows? My mother was asleep. No phone is gonna wake her up."

"Was Susan home?"

"You sound like a fuckin' cop."

She was right. I was so intent on trying to find out what happened I lost sight of what Cynthia must have been going through. This wasn't the time to ask questions. I reached into my back pocket, took out my wallet and held out two twenties. "It's not much," I said. "But maybe it'll help. Tell your mother I'm sorry."

She looked at the bills for a few seconds. "Don't need your money." She went back inside and slammed the door.

"Bitch," I muttered under my breath.

I went back to my car, sat and stared at the house. Cynthia's mood swings seemed too dramatic. Like an actress playing a role. Why would she want me to think Petey was evil? I hadn't gotten the sense that Susan thought he was dangerous the night we talked at the coffee shop. She kept saying that Petey was a good kid.

I had gotten to know Petey pretty well. I didn't see him as a con man, and I certainly didn't think of him as evil. Impulsive, sure. I had seen him act out many times without regard to the consequences, but I had also seen him really interested in doing well on his school work. "It's my only way out of that neighborhood," he had told me.

Maybe Cynthia was just affected by the shock of everything that happened.

I sat for awhile longer, then started my car. A dark, blue beat-up Ford Escort slowly drove by me and pulled into a parking space further up the street.

The curtains in the house parted and Cynthia looked out of the living room window. A few seconds later the front door opened. I expected her to come out onto the porch, but she stood in the door-way and motioned toward the person in the Escort.

The driver didn't move. I pulled away from the curb slowly and when I got parallel to the car I glanced in. The driver turned away as if he didn't want to be seen. A streetlight illuminated the inside of the car. His expensive suit looked out of place in the old car.

I took a right and watched him in my mirror. I wondered why he didn't want me to see him. I circled the block, killed my lights and sat a few houses down from the Olivers. The driver remained in the car.

I waited. Several minutes passed. Then he got out and moved quickly across the sidewalk. When he passed under a streetlight I saw that his jacket collar was pulled up and he wore wrap-around sunglasses even though it was dark. I almost laughed. He reminded me of someone trying to impersonate a secret agent.

I drove slowly toward the house and turned on my headlights. They shined on him for an instant. He turned away and walked toward the Olivers' steps. In that brief moment I realized that I knew him. It would be hard not to recognize the man whom most opinion polls said would be elected the next governor of Massachusetts.

CHAPTER 5

He moved quickly up the porch steps and went inside.

I stared at the house. There was no doubt in my mind who it was. I had seen him on television many times and pictures of him, his wife and three kids seemed always to be in the paper. I had even met him. So why was he sneaking into the Olivers' house?

Edward McKinley had been a state senator for the past twenty years. Six months ago he announced his candidacy for governor. If he could get his party's nomination he would be elected. Most saw it as a stepping stone to higher office.

I made a U-turn and drove around for awhile, thinking. I needed to get rid of my nervous energy.

I'd worked on political campaigns for different candidates and that was how I'd met McKinley. I never liked him. Seeing him brought my feelings to the surface. To me, he seemed too smooth. The type who was swayed by political polls and didn't have any real convictions. His constituents considered him a good family man with strong values. He kept getting re-elected, and during his time in the Senate had done a lot of favors for people. He seemed to be calling them in.

Abraham Lincoln had said, "Politicians are a set of men who have interests aside from the interests of the people." McKinley was a good example of what he meant.

I thought about stopping at the homeless shelter where I did volunteer work, but didn't feel up to telling about my discovery of Susan's body again. I decided to go home and clean up the kitchen. At least I'd feel like I was accomplishing something. When I got back the lock on the door had been repaired.

The message light on my answering machine was flashing. I pressed the retrieve button. A reporter from The Boston Globe had called wanting to talk about Susan. There were also several hang-ups. I erased the message and went into the kitchen.

It was spotless. I smiled and shook my head. Broken dishes and glasses were piled in a box on the floor. What was salvageable had been put back on the shelves. The floor had been washed.

I turned to Richard. "Did you do this or has Dave been at work again?"

Richard cocked his head. He would have taken credit for it if he could.

I put on a Dion C.D. and sat on the couch. Music relaxed me and listening to oldies brought me back to a time when things were less stressful. I was just getting into "The Wanderer" when the phone rang.

"Steve, it's Aaron Fleming. I've been trying to get you all night."

Aaron was a reporter for the Waltham News Tribune, our city's excuse for a newspaper. I had met him a few times at local functions and he had interviewed me once about a recycling plan that I had set up at school. One year we played on the same team in the Waltham Adult Basketball League. His reporting had always been fair and I liked him.

"Before you ask," I said. "I don't have anything I want to say."

"Steve," he said. "Remember when I set you up with Rhonda?"

I laughed. "You didn't set me up. You introduced me to her at a bar."

"Same thing," he said. "I need a favor. The police aren't saying anything about Susan's death. I've got a story to write and if I just rehash what's already been written my editor's going to be pissed. A few things, that's all I need."

"You're going from covering school board meetings to handling a murder," I said. "That's quite a jump."

"Hey, I had to convince my editor I was the person for this story. I told him I knew Susan and that you and I are old friends."

"I never realized we were such good buddies," I said. "Okay, you can quote me on this. No comment."

"Let me buy you a drink. We'll talk off the record if you want. This could be a major break for me. I'd owe you big time."

I sighed. I wasn't in the mood to argue and I didn't want to meet him for a drink. A favor Aaron could do for me flashed into my mind. "Okay," I said. "But I've got something I want you to check on for me."

"Anything you want."

I gave him the abbreviated version of how I found Susan's body.

"Jesus," he said. "This is great stuff. When I add it to what I know about Susan it's going to be a hell of a story. You won't regret it, buddy."

"Now it's your turn," I said. "I just came from the Oliver house. Any idea why Edward McKinley would be visiting them?"

"Did he have a camera crew and was he saying things like when I'm elected Governor this kind of violence won't happen?"

"He was alone," I said.

"Doesn't sound like McKinley," Aaron said. "I think I'll take a ride over there and see what's going on. I'll let you know. Thanks, Steve."

I hung up, turned the C.D. player up louder and plopped down on the couch.

The next thing I knew it was seven a.m. I stretched and walked into the kitchen. "Morning, Richard," I said filling the coffeemaker. "How do you want your eggs today?"

Richard clucked, then whistled softly.

I popped a bagel into the toaster. When it was done I slathered it with cream cheese, put lox on it, a Bermuda onion over that and topped it with sliced tomato. I was working on my second cup of coffee when I heard the sound of the Globe delivery truck dropping off the paper. I went out to the front yard and retrieved it.

The first thing I saw when I spread it on the living room floor was the picture of a smiling Susan Oliver. I studied her face. Young, attractive, flowing blonde hair. An image of her bloodied face suddenly popped into my mind. I pushed my coffee cup aside.

I skimmed the story. It mentioned I had found Susan's body, but didn't say I was a suspect. Most of what was printed I knew. The only new information I learned was that Susan's ex-husband had been questioned for a few hours and released. The police claimed he wasn't a suspect.

"Great. Now they'll be focusing on me," I said aloud.

Inside the paper was a story on Susan's life. It told of her growing up as one of four children in a poor family. Susan's mother stayed home to raise the kids, and her father was in and out of work. Susan attended the University of Massachusetts on an art scholarship, but dropped out when her father left home. She took a job as a waitress to help support the family. It mentioned her unsuccessful six-month marriage, the death of her younger brother, Dwight, and the disappearance of Petey.

Under that was a story about the search for Petey. It was accompanied by a picture that must have been taken when he was ten. He tried to give a tough-guy stare. It didn't work.

I was reading the sports page when the phone rang. It was Aaron Fleming.

"I checked out the McKinley thing," he said. "He wasn't at the Olivers when I arrived, and Susan's sister, Cynthia, told me he never was there and she didn't even know who he was. She was pretty rude. Said the only guy that had been there all night was Petey's asshole teacher."

"She must have been talking about one of Petey's other asshole teachers," I said.

"Anyway, I called McKinley's press secretary a couple of times, but he hasn't returned my calls. According to his press calendar he was speaking at the Newton Women's League last night. You sure it was him?"

"I'm sure," I said. "Newton's only five minutes away. He could have ducked out for a few minutes and gone over to the Olivers."

"Why would the Olivers deny it?" Aaron said.

"I don't know. I do know that Cynthia was expecting him. She was at the door waiting for him and McKinley was acting like he didn't want to be seen. He even drove a beat-up Ford Escort. Might be an interesting story if you could find out why."

"You kidding? It would be a great story. Especially if he's trying to hide it. "

"I just hope McKinley's not planning on making Susan's death a campaign issue. That family's been through so much they might agree to do anything that sleazy politician asks."

"I'll make a few more phone calls. See what I can find out. Then I'll talk to McKinley."

I put on an Everly Brothers album and went back to the paper. I had trouble concentrating. My conversation with Aaron kept nagging at me. Why would Cynthia deny McKinley was at the house? Stories about his political ambition were legendary. He had never hesitated to step on a few people during his rise if it suited his purpose. My instincts told me he was up to something and it involved the Olivers. The family had suffered enough. Maybe I was wrong, but I had to know. I didn't want to wait for Aaron. I'd check it out myself.

I called information, got the number for The McKinley for Governor Committee and dialed it. The worker who answered told me that they were open and I should drop in. "We're always looking for volunteers," she said, "and yes, Mr. McKinley usually stops by before he goes out on the campaign trail. Should be in within the hour." She had so much enthusiasm I thought I had made one of the most momentous decisions of my life.

It was cold and sunny as I backed out of the driveway. A nice day for a drive into Boston.

My mother had always said: "Never do business over the phone that you can conduct in person." I had followed her advice many times and it usually worked.

I circled Boston Common, then parked next to the Public Gardens and walked along the path which led through it. A few people sat on benches while others strolled. The sun reflected off the water where the Swan Boats sailed in the summer. I gazed at the Ritz Carlton across the street and had a sudden urge for a Bloody Mary.

The McKinley Headquarters was located on Tremont Street. It's lights were on as were the tobacconist's and the jeweler's on either side. Large campaign posters hung in the window. I studied his face. Rugged looking, toothy grin, tussled hair. He appeared younger than his forty plus years. If you voted on looks alone, McKinley would be elected.

I peered in the window. A woman with gray hair was sitting at a brown metal desk, talking on the telephone. Several other phones lined the desk. A man in shirtsleeves stood at a copying machine. He wore dark rimmed glasses and his hair was cropped short.

I went in and approached the gray haired woman. She looked up, smiled and held up one finger. She appeared to be in her mid-fifties. I glanced around the office. Several long tables were covered with 'McKinley for Governor' signs. Another table held a computer and a fax machine. The copy machine whirred and spit out papers. The man at the copier didn't look up.

When the woman hung up I introduced myself.

Her smile got wider. "I'm Meg, Steve," she said. "You got here pretty quickly. I could use some help if you're interested in making phone calls." She handed me a paper. "This is all you have to say."

I looked at it. "Ed is a man of real integrity," I read aloud.

The man at the copy machine looked over and smiled. We were like one happy family.

"He's wonderful," she said. "Have you ever met him?"

"Actually I saw him at the Olivers' house last night," I said. "Susan Oliver was killed at Walden Pond Friday night. You might have read about it. Her brother, Petey, is missing. I was curious about what Mr. McKinley was doing there."

Meg squinted and put her hand on her chin. "Mr. McKinley spoke to the Newton Women's League last night," she said. "He didn't visit the Olivers."

"Really," I said. "When I saw him it seemed like he didn't want to be recognized. What time do you expect him in?"

She hesitated. "I'm not sure."

"You said on the phone he'd be here within the hour. I'll wait."

"Are you a friend of the woman's?"

"I am. I'm also the one who found her body."

The man at the copy machine turned. I had his full attention now.

Meg's eyes narrowed. "You didn't come here to help Mr. McKinley," she said. "Are you from the press?"

I shook my head. "I'm just curious about what he was doing. I figured I'd ask him personally. Was Susan a friend of his?"

The man from the copy machine turned and walked in my direction. "I was with Ed last night," he said. "He attended a fundraiser and came straight back here. It was after midnight. What kind of bullshit are you trying to spread?"

"I saw him at the Olivers about nine o' clock."

"I was with him at nine."

"He was alone."

Meg got up from her chair. "I'm going to have to ask you to leave," she said.

The man took another step in my direction.

Several folding chairs were lined up to my right. I sat down in one. "Just ignore me. I'm fine. Really."

"You want me to call the cops?" the man said. "We've asked you to leave. Far as I'm concerned you're trespassing."

I got up, smiled at him then turned to Meg. "Okay," I said. "I was hoping to talk to McKinley in person, but would you ask him to call me?" When she didn't respond I turned and left.

I looked back through the window. Meg and the copy machine man were talking. Then she picked up the phone and dialed. Her eyes narrowed and her expression was determined as she talked. Maybe she had called McKinley to tell him about me.

I hung around on Tremont Street for over an hour hoping to spot McKinley. Why would his organization cover for him? Maybe I should just head home. Tomorrow I could go back to teaching. The cops will find Susan's murderer and I'd be left alone. That's what I really wanted. But everyone denying McKinley was at the house made me more determined to know why he was there. I waited awhile longer, then left. I'd meet up with McKinley later.

Back at my apartment, I searched the paper for any stories on McKinley. A small article noted his appearance in Newton the previous night where he emphasized his war on crime. He didn't mention Susan Oliver. I was about to make coffee when the doorbell rang.

I walked over to the window and looked out. Lieutenant Nash was standing on the front steps. I thought about my lawyer friend, Lisa Gerrault. Why hadn't she returned my phone call? I went down and let him in.

He walked into the kitchen, looked around then focused on Richard's cage. "A parakeet. What a great pet," he said. "Can he talk?"

"You kidding. He sings. Knows the entire Elvis songbook."

Nash put his nose inches from the cage and peered in. Richard cocked his head. Nash poked the cage with his finger and Richard hopped along his perch toward him.

"Maybe I should get a parakeet," Nash said. "My wife always says she wants a pet."

"Richard's great." I said. "Politically we agree on everything except he believes in the death penalty for hunters."

Nash tugged on the sleeve of his sport jacket. His tie hung loose and the collar of his white shirt was frayed. "Sorry to bother you on a Sunday, but I had a few questions I wanted to ask about the Oliver girl."

"You want some coffee," I said. "I was just about to make some."

"No, No. I'm fine. Just ate lunch." He patted his stomach.

"I can't tell you anymore then I did the other night."

"I need you to clear up a couple of things for me," he said. "You said you only knew her slightly and had gone out once. Is that right?"

I nodded. "I saw her a couple of times at school and we went out once, had coffee and talked about Petey."

He looked at me as if he expected more. Then he shrugged. "Her friends say different. They say you two were dating. Had been dating for a few months. That she was always talking about you. She told them you made a move on her at school. One of them thought you two had a date the night she was killed."

"That's not true," I said.

He coughed and pulled out his handkerchief. "Sorry," he said. He wiped his nose then put the handkerchief back in his pocket. "Which part isn't true? That you weren't dating or you didn't see her the night she was killed."

"All of it," I said.

"She told her friends she spent a lot of nights here at your place."

"Lieutenant, I have a woman in my life," I said. "She was here when Petey called."

"Could you tell me how to reach her?"

I gave him Beth's number, then said, "I don't know what Susan's told people, but I'm telling you nothing happened. Did any of her friends see us together?"

He shook his head. "Susan told them you wanted it that way. You thought it would look bad if people saw you with a much younger woman who was the sister of a student. You being a teacher and all."

"Susan was twenty-eight," I said. "If I had dated her I wouldn't have hidden it. This is crazy."

"She was twenty-five," he said.

"Her age doesn't make a difference. We never dated."

He shrugged. "Right now all I know is what people tell me. I'm gonna check everything out, but I figured I'd ask you."

"Thank you. Once you've looked into it you'll see it's not true." I hesitated. "Reporter from The Herald said I was a major suspect."

He smiled. It looked out of place. "Lots of people are suspects till I find out differently."

"Did you learn anything from Susan's ex-husband."

He smiled again. "You don't really expect me to discuss the investigation with you? You'll find out what I know soon enough." He glanced around the room. "You wouldn't have any objection to us checking your apartment for fingerprints, would you?"

"My place was broken into Friday night and the Waltham Police already checked," I said. "You can call them."

"Anything taken?"

"Just my collection of videos."

"What kind of videos?"

"Just a few movies and a blank tape."

He paused for a few seconds, then his eyes locked on mine. "One thing you might be interested in," he said. "We just got the results of the autopsy. Susan Oliver was pregnant."

CHAPTER 6

When Nash left I dialed my lawyer friend, Lisa Gerrault. Still no answer. She must be away for the weekend. Then I tried to sit, but couldn't stay still. I paced around the living room. I opened my liquor cabinet, looked at my bottle of scotch, but decided I didn't need it. I sat in a chair, decided the one by the window was better, then rejected both and stretched out on the couch. Richard remained quiet as if he could sense something was wrong. I remembered the cop who questioned me twenty years ago. Compared to his interrogation Nash's questioning appeared mild, but his good-guy routine had grated on me. He was investigating me and I didn't like it.

Nash's words kept circling around in my brain. You'll find out what I know soon enough, he had said. What the hell did that mean? I replayed finding Susan's body in my mind. I had been there when it happened, for Chrissake. If I had moved more quickly could I have stopped it? If I had called the cops when Petey called, Susan might still be alive. The more I thought the more frustration I felt. It was the same feeling I had when Mitch died. I shook my head. Whoever killed Susan was still walking free, and by her lying about our relationship Nash was wasting his time on me. Why would she tell her friends we dated? Could she have been setting me up to explain her pregnancy?

If I'd been thinking clearly I would have told Nash about McKinley. Let him find out why he visited the Olivers. I'd tell him later. I had the feeling I'd be talking to him again.

I reached for the phone to call Beth, but then remembered she was in Rockport.

I needed to clear my head. I put my jacket on and walked out to the front yard. The sky was milky white and a brisk breeze moved through the tree branches. I zipped my jacket up, got into my car and started to drive.

I meandered through the city, then drove onto Route 128 and stepped on the accelerator. Before I realized it I was on Route 2. I found myself heading toward Walden.

I pulled off the road next to a no parking barricade in front of the pond, stared at the bathhouse and out onto the water. I closed my eyes for a few seconds. Then I got out of the car and walked down the black-topped path. The cool wind chilled me and I pulled my jacket collar up. A few people strolled on the path which led around the pond. A couple sat, bundled up, on the cement wall. They waved at me.

I stared out across the water. Dark clouds had started to form overhead making the pond a dark slate gray color. Soft ripples moved across it. I'd been a kid when I first came to Walden. As I grew older I pictured myself married and bringing my own kids here. It hadn't worked out. Beth and I decided to wait a few years before having a family and by that time we were hardly speaking. Sometimes when I looked at kids like Petey I felt a sense of disappointment that I'd never had any of my own. Thing was, it wasn't too late.

I picked up a stone and skimmed it along the surface of the water, then headed down the path to where I had found Susan's body. The area was deserted. No police guarding the site. No yellow tape marking it as a crime scene. The only indication of the violence that had happened were scuffed footprints in the dirt. I felt a knot form in my stomach.

The wire fence was still down and I sat on the slope. I thought about Petey and how he started to hang around in my room after school.

The first couple of weeks Petey didn't say much in class and sometimes didn't seem to be paying attention. But he always knew the answer when I called on him. His answers tended to be more analytical than factual. He told me his two heroes were Martin Luther King and John F. Kennedy. Pretty good choices for a kid of thirteen. I was surprised to find out he was a major discipline problem in other classes. The principal said he was one of the most difficult kids in the school.

I'd see him walking in the corridor, surrounded by friends, laughing and talking loudly. He had a rebellious streak that reminded me of myself at his age. I checked into his background and found that most teachers found him hard to handle, but felt that he was exceptionally bright. His grades didn't reflect it. I began to take an interest in him.

It was the end of September. I had been teaching a class for ten minutes when I heard a knock on the door. It was Petey.

"I need a late pass, Mr. A." He gave me a sheepish grin. "I was thirty seconds late for Mr. Haskell's class."

He wore a Kurt Cobain T-shirt and faded jeans torn at the knee. His brown hair was slicked back, but a few strands fell over his forehead. He squinted at me.

I pointed at his shirt. "Kurt could be your brother," I said. "You look alike."

His smile grew wider. It transformed him. Made him look younger. "The pass, Mr. A."

"You left here on time."

"Yeah, well his room is on the other end of the building. You know how crowded the halls get. Not everyone wants to get to class on time like I do."

"If you stopped talking to all the girls who belong to your fan club you would have made it."

"That's what I like about you. You always understand. I bet you were just like me in school."

"Matter of fact I was, except for the having girls all over me part. But when I was late I got punished. Explain it to Mr. Haskell. He'll understand."

He looked away. "He won't listen. If I get any more demerits they're going to suspend me. My sister will kill me."

I shrugged. "Next time run."

He turned back. "Okay," he said. "I was five minutes late. I had to go to the bathroom. It was an emergency."

I smiled, went into my room, wrote out a pass and handed it to him. "I'm doing you a favor just this time. From now on if you're late you'll have to take the consequences."

"Thanks, Mr. A.," he said, then turned and walked up the hallway. "Next time I'll con some other teacher," he mumbled.

One week later he started hanging around in my classroom.

He often talked about his relationship with his family and his dream of being a major-league baseball player. His mother was sickly, couldn't work and left the real discipline to Susan. Susan and Petey were both stubborn and often clashed, but I never had the sense he hated her. I felt his need to talk and straighten things out in his mind. I tried to help him. That's when I gave him my phone number.

"Where the hell are you, Petey?" I said aloud.

I'm not sure how long I sat by the pond, but when I got back to my apartment it was almost two.

There was a message on my machine. I punched the button.

"The police are releasing Susan's body tomorrow," Cynthia Oliver said. "Just thought you'd like to know, Mr. Teacher. If you talk to Petey you might want to tell him the funeral's on Wednesday." I could hear the anger in her voice.

The next couple of hours were hazy. Several friends called, some from school, some from around town who had read about what had happened. I spent twenty minutes on the phone with my mother. It took awhile to convince her I was fine.

I watched a football game for awhile, but had trouble focusing on what was happening. It ended just after four p.m. It felt much later.

The ringing of the doorbell jolted me. I walked to the window. A man stood with his back to the door. He was about my age, tall with brown close cropped hair. He had on a dark blue suit. He rang the bell again. His face looked vaguely familiar.

I focused on his car. It was a late model, white Lincoln Continental. I went down and opened the door. The chain lock held it in place. "Can I help you?" I said.

He squinted and leaned forward. "I'm looking for Steve Asher."

"If you're from the press I don't have any comment."

"No, no." He gave me a toothy grin and blinked several times. "Could you come with me. Edward McKinley wants to talk to you. It'll only take about an hour and it'll clear some things up for you."

"Why didn't Mr. McKinley come here himself?" I said.

"He'd like to talk privately."

"Is it about his visit to the Olivers last night?"

"I don't know, sir," he said. "He didn't tell me."

"Look," I said. "I don't have time for games. I just want some honest answers. You can start by telling me who you are."

"James Carberry. I'm Mr. McKinley's press secretary."

I realized that I had seen this man on television a few times. He had worked for McKinley's Democratic opponent, Frank Mitchell, for awhile, but had left that campaign to join the McKinley bandwagon. "Give me a number where I can reach him," I said. "If he verifies what you say, I'll meet him."

He reached into his pocket, pulled out a billfold then slipped a card through the door. "It's his car phone," he said.

I shut the door, went upstairs and dialed. After one ring it was answered.

"Edward McKinley," he said.

"Mr. McKinley, this is Steve Asher. You'd like to talk to me?"

"Yes, Mr. Asher," he said. "Please, it's important. I'm sorry for the inconvenience, but I'm taking a chance even talking to you."

It sounded like his voice, but I wanted him to say more.

"I saw you at the Olivers last night," I said.

"I know. I don't want any misunderstandings." He hesitated. "Please."

When I hung up I was certain that I had just talked to Edward McKinley. I wondered why he didn't just say he had gone to the Olivers to offer his sympathy. I wouldn't have believed him, but it was an answer. Why this need to talk to me?. I grabbed my jacket and headed down the stairs.

Carberry was leaning against his car when I walked out of the house. "Will you come now?" he said.

I nodded and headed toward my car.

"You can drive with me," he said. "I'll take you back."

"I'll drive my own car, thanks."

I backed out of the driveway and slowly followed James Carberry up the street.

CHAPTER 7

The Charles River meanders through Waltham. It's part of what gives the city character. Factories had been built along its banks during the 1800s. During the depression many of them closed. Recently some had been turned into apartment buildings, but there was still plenty of vacant land along the shore.

Carberry drove over the river then took a right into the Mount Feake Cemetery. It was a spacious area with rolling hills. More like a park then a place for burying people. The sun reflected off the river. On the opposite shore was the old watch factory. Carberry pulled behind a late model Ford and stopped.

In the distance I could see McKinley sitting on the grass, his back resting against a maple tree, staring out at the water. A piece of straw hung from his mouth. When he heard Carberry's door slam he got up and stared in my direction.

He was in his late-forties, but his dark hair and good looks made him appear younger. He wore jeans, cowboy boots, a western shirt and the same wrap-around sun glasses that he had on the last time I'd seen him.

He had played basketball for B.C. and had a tryout with the Celtics. He still had that lean, athletic body. It was forty-five degrees outside and he didn't wear a jacket.

As I walked toward him I glanced back at Carberry. He was leaning against the car, staring straight ahead as if we didn't exist.

McKinley waited until I reached him, then extended his hand. "I appreciate your coming, Steve." He took his sunglasses off and put them in his shirt pocket. "It must have been terrible finding Susan's body that way. I can only imagine what it was like. I've got a daughter her age."

"It was," I said.

"Senator Kelly speaks highly of you. Told me about all the work you did on his last campaign. Said you're intelligent and level-headed." He stopped talking and looked toward a Cadillac which pulled onto the road. It slowed as it passed us, then sped by.

"Is that why you wanted to meet with me? To tell me how smart I was?"

He shook his head. "I want to talk about Susan. You knew her. I need to know what was bothering her before she died. She was acting strangely. I figured you'd be a good person to ask."

"Where'd you hear Susan and I were such good friends?"

He shrugged. "Her sister might have mentioned it."

"I only met Susan once and we talked about her brother, Petey. He's one of my students."

"I know. I talked to Mrs. Oliver about him last night. Damn shame what the family's going through."

I nodded. "So why all the secrecy about you going to their house?"

"That's one of the things I want to talk to you about."

I waited for him to say more. When he didn't I said. "What was Susan doing that was so strange?"

"Maybe it'll make more sense if I tell you a story. Perhaps you could give me some advice."

"I'm sure you have plenty of people who give you advice," I said, "but I'd be glad to listen."

He gazed out at the river, took a deep breath then turned back to me. "I met Susan about four months ago. I was with my staff having a business meeting and she was our waitress. She told me she supported me, liked what I stood for." He hesitated for a few seconds. "I told her she should work for the campaign. I gave her my card and told her to call the office, something I've done hundreds of times before. That's when the calls started coming. Just a few at first, but she got more persistent. She wanted to meet with me privately. She'd say things like, 'I saw you on television', or 'you're a beautiful man'. I'd see her in the crowd when I was speaking. I can't describe the look on her face, but it frightened me. I felt like she was stalking me."

"Why didn't you tell her to knock it off? That's what I would've done."

He shook his head. "I thought she'd stop. When she didn't I gave my staff orders to tell her not to call." He motioned toward Carberry. "I even sent Jim to talk to her, but it didn't work. She called my office eighteen times in one day, always giving her name and saying it was important that she talk to me. Steve, I have a wife and three great kids." He took a few steps along the shore.

"What does this have to do with me?" I said.

"I need to get a handle on why she was doing this and how far she was planning on going with it."

"What's the point? Susan's dead. And besides, I didn't know her that well."

"I've heard otherwise."

"I don't care what you've heard."

"Then you've got an idea what I'm going through. Susan's been telling stories about me. That's why I went to the Olivers last night. I had no idea what she told them. I wanted to set things straight."

"What had she told them?"

"That she was working for me and I had taken a special interest in her. Claimed I had promised her a job if I were elected. None of it's true." He sighed and shook his head. "It's more than politics, here. I'm thinking about what these rumors could do to my family. I could use your help."

"I don't even know why you're telling me this, but I'll be glad to give you some advice. I'd be open about what happened. Tell people what you told me before it comes out and makes it look like you tried to hide it."

He looked out at the water for a few seconds. "Frank Mitchell's got as much chance of getting the nomination as I do. If he finds out about this his people will run with it. Hell, he'd just love to spread a few rumors that bring my character into question."

"I thought this wasn't about politics. Look, your staff was aware of the phone calls. Susan could have mentioned you to some of her friends. Any one of them could tell the press. You've got to face facts. It's going to come out."

"That's what makes it so frustrating," he said. "None of it's true. You can see what I'm going through, can't you Steve? I've worked so hard."

I shrugged. "Why did you really want to meet with me?"

"To ask you about Susan."

"I don't think so. I think you want me to keep my mouth shut about what I saw."

His eyes narrowed and for the first time I saw real anger. "That's not what this is about. You do what you have to do. I just want you to know the truth. You want to know what bothers me? I keep thinking about the Susan who waited on us at the restaurant. She was young, attractive and intelligent. Something happened to change her. I don't know what. I was hoping you could help me understand. You can be cynical if you want, but I'd like to help the Olivers cope with their loss."

"Sorry," I said. "I can't tell you any more than I have."

I looked out at the water and wondered what I would do if the press started to report some of the things Susan had said about me. "Are the Olivers going to the media?" I said.

He shook his head. "They were very understanding. It may sound cruel, but Susan is dead. There's nothing we can do about that. We've got to think of the future and how to prevent this type of tragedy from happening again."

"Sounds like a political speech," I said.

He looked away. When he turned back he was frowning. "Maybe, but I really believe in what I'm doing. I appreciate your coming." He looked toward Carberry and raised one finger. When I looked over the press secretary was heading toward us.

I turned back to McKinley. "Did you know that Susan was pregnant?" I said.

Color drained from his face. "Jesus, no," he said. "That's just horrible. The poor family." He hesitated then reached out his hand. "Thanks for meeting me, Steve."

I stared at him for a few seconds, then turned, walked by Carberry and headed toward my car. I made a U-turn and slowly pulled out onto the main street. As I drove by, they were staring at me.

I opened the car window and breathed in the cold air. I had this nagging feeling that McKinley hadn't told me the real reason for our meeting. I should call Nash and tell him about the conversation. The thing was, if McKinley was innocent and Susan had been lying about him, I knew how he felt.

By the time I got home the sun had just started to set. Dave's lights were on in his apartment. Sometimes I stopped in to say hello. Tonight I wanted to be alone.

The message light on my machine was blinking. I pressed the button. Beth had come back early and wanted to go out for a drink. Suddenly being alone was less attractive. I called her and made arrangements to meet.

I had to tell Beth about Susan's claim that we'd dated before she heard it from someone else. She'd been jealous of other women when we were married. I didn't know how she'd react to Susan's lies.

The bar at the Iguana Cantina was a Brandeis students' hang-out. Beth was sitting at the bar drinking a Margarita and watching a football game when I arrived. She was thirty-six, but looked younger. She wore a black skirt and a cranberry blouse. Her blonde hair fell to her shoulders. She turned toward me and smiled. In that split second I realized how much like Susan Oliver she looked.

She draped her arm on my shoulder and kissed me on the cheek. "I came back early to make sure you're okay."

I smiled. "I'm glad you did."

She stared at me for a few seconds. "You didn't want to talk about finding Susan yesterday. If you're ready to talk now I'll listen."

"You always did like to talk everything out."

"It helps."

"I've relived it so many times in my head, but it always comes out the same." I glanced up at the television for a few seconds. "How was Rockport?"

"Fine," she said. "Sold a couple of paintings and met an old friend of ours. You remember Linda Turcotte?"

I nodded.

"She asked about you. When I told her we were divorced but had started dating again, she looked at me as if I were crazy."

"You never did have good taste in men."

I ordered a Margarita, dipped a nacho into the salsa, and shoveled it into my mouth. I realized I hadn't eaten since breakfast. I watched a college student flex his muscle while the girl across from him smiled, then I refocused on Beth. "Next to the ravages of war and natural catastrophes," I said, "singles bars are third on my list of things that I never want to be involved with."

She smiled. "Part of your charm is that you still use phrases like singles bars." She looked toward the couple, then back at me. I could tell by her expression that something was on her mind.

"What's wrong?" I said.

She shrugged. "It's kinda scary getting involved with you again. It didn't work the first time."

"Hey," I said. "This is the new Steve Asher. Six years older and much more mature." I wrapped the Margarita straw around my ear.

Beth smiled then frowned. "You never did like to talk about anything serious. Is it stupid for us to try and make this work again?"

I shook my head. "I think we both learned some things. We're gonna do it better this time."

We sat in silence for a few minutes as I pretended to focus on the football game. Things had been going so well for us lately and I really wanted our relationship to work. There was so much I wanted to say to her about us, but I was afraid if we talked Beth might go away again. Instead, when I turned back to her I talked about seeing McKinley at the Olivers, my meeting with him this afternoon and Susan being pregnant.

"Is McKinley a suspect in Susan's murder?"

"I don't know," I said.

"I always thought the guy was scum," she said. "He probably knocked her up and now he's trying to save his political career."

I looked back at the football game for a few seconds. "Couldn't Susan be the one lying?"

"Why? So she could get her name in the papers."

"Sure. She'd become an instant celebrity. Hell, Julia Roberts could play her in the movie."

"I'd rather see Jamie Lee Curtis."

"Me too, but she's not right for Susan's part."

The bartender came over and asked Beth if she wanted another drink. She shook her head. When he left I said, "Susan told some of her friends that we were dating."

She rubbed her finger along the rim of her glass. "Were you?"

"There you go again. No I wasn't."

"You've mentioned her a few times to me. Didn't you go out and have coffee with her?"

"Yeah, to talk about Petey, but she told people that we dated a lot.

It pisses me off that she lied."

"Were you attracted to her?"

I hesitated. "Yeah."

"Did you want to screw her?"

I shook my head. I felt guilty because I had thought about going to bed with Susan. If things didn't work out with Beth, maybe I would have asked her out.

Now she's dead.

"Can we stop this?" I said.

She nodded. "So who'd play you in the movie? I got it. Bill Murray. Nah he's too good looking to play you."

I studied her face for a few seconds. "I was thinking more along the lines of Kevin Costner."

"Now that's funny."

We talked awhile longer. I had another Margarita. "You wanna come over?" I said finishing my drink.

"Not tonight. I need some private time. I just wanted to make sure you were all right."

I put my hand over hers. "Thanks."

She squeezed my hand. "I'll be right back." She kissed me lightly on the lips, swiveled off the stool and walked toward the ladies room.

Beth and I had trouble right from the beginning of our four-year marriage. She became jealous over non-existent affairs and frustrated with the amount of time I spent at school. I didn't want to deal with the problem, and after four years she had had it. We decided to go to Barbados to try and work things out. I thought a week of sun, sex, food and Pina Coladas could help our marriage work. It was a lot for a week in the Caribbean to cure. By the end of it we were hardly speaking, and by the time we got back to Boston we both knew it was over.

We made an attempt a couple of times to try to make things work again, but we were through. When we had dinner a few months ago we realized that both of us had changed. We decided to try one more time. I still loved this woman.

We held hands as I walked her to her car. Then I watched her drive away. I wondered if she believed what I had told her about Susan.

The message light on my machine was flashing when I got home. I reached over and pressed the retrieve button.

"Mr. Asher?" It was Petey's voice. "I just wanted you to know that I'm all right." He hung up.

CHAPTER 8

"Thank, God," I said.

I woke up the next morning with a headache. I had tossed and turned most of the night. I kept hoping the phone would ring, it would be Petey and he'd tell me where he was, but at least I knew he was still alive.

I fumbled through my shower, wolfed down some Cheerios then left a message for Rita telling her about Petey's call.

A cold drizzle was falling when I pointed my car in the direction of school.

North Middle School had been built in the fifties. It was a brick two-story structure that sat back from the main road and was surrounded by trees on all sides with a small pond in front. A soccer field was in the back.

The minute I walked in the door I could tell that it wasn't going to be a normal day.

As I collected my mail in the main office, several teachers surrounded me. Most offered support and said they would have done the same thing if Petey had called them. Their words made me feel better. Others avoided me and conversations would end as I approached. They'd give me a polite smile and walk away. It made me feel uneasy.

My classes were different, too. The most difficult part of my day is usually settling down my students, getting them into their seats and ready to learn. Today they sat quietly, their eyes focused on me as I entered the classroom. I never realized how much I enjoyed their chatter.

Billy Anderson raised his hand. "Mr. A.," he said. "You gonna tell us about finding the body?"

I shook my head. "It's not something I want to relive, but as bad as it was for me to find Susan, it's worse for Petey and his family."

"Was it all bloody?" he asked.

"You're a jerk," the girl next to him said.

"Wait a minute," I said. "Billy asked what many of you are probably thinking. Thing is, most of you have had some kind of experience in your lives that you don't want to talk about. I wouldn't ask you to discuss it if you didn't want to. I hope you respect me enough to do the same. One thing we can all do is let the Olivers know how we feel about Susan's death and hope that Petey comes home soon."

Each class that arrived asked the same questions. I described my feelings and my concern for the Oliver family. I avoided graphic details, which disappointed most of them. For a day I was a celebrity in their eyes.

At one point I ran into the teacher who had argued with Petey just before he had run out of school last Wednesday. I had heard what had happened, but asked her to tell me about it. She had seen him in the hallway between classes. He appeared distraught. When she asked him if everything was all right, he told her to "fuck off." She told him to report to the office and he swore again, then ran out of the building. Petey may be rebellious and stubborn, but this type of conduct seemed out of character even for him.

Between classes I went to my mailbox. There was a message to call Aaron Fleming. I slipped his number into my shirt pocket.

The rumor reached me about mid-day. Ralph Tompkins, the English Teacher in the next room, stuck his head into my class. "There's a police officer in the building," he said. "He's asking questions about you."

It didn't make my day any better.

My mind flashed to Lisa Gerrault. She must be in her office by now. I should call and not talk to Nash until I have. I shook my head. I've already talked to him twice. What could he possibly ask me about today?

Fifteen minutes later, just as I was getting ready to go to lunch, I heard a sneeze and then footsteps in the corridor. A knot tightened in my stomach. As the footsteps approached I yelled, "Come in, Lieutenant."

He poked his head into the room, stopped and smiled. "The

sneeze, right?" He wiped his nose with his handkerchief, then stuck it in his sport coat pocket.

I pointed to my forehead. "Actually I'm psychic." I motioned him in and he closed the door.

"This weather's killing me," he said shaking his head.

I sat on my desk while he stood opposite me. He glanced at my bulletin board. His blue sport coat pulled tight around his stomach. "History," he said. "I used to love history when I was in school." Then he turned to me. "I don't really like questioning teachers with the kids around, but it's the only time I could get all of you together. I wanted some information on the Oliver kid." He shrugged. "A lot of people were very willing to tell me things about you."

"Such as?"

He scratched the back of his head. "You're not exactly Mr. Popularity with some of the faculty."

I nodded. When I had been the Teacher's Union Representative I had supported stronger evaluations of teachers. It had been controversial, and some of the faculty opposed it and still felt resentment toward me.

"They tell me you like to cause trouble around here. The principal has had to talk to you several times."

I felt like a kid being scolded. "Look," I said. "It's lunch time and I'm hungry. I know I'm one of your suspects. I didn't do it. If you're asking questions about Petey, you're wasting your time. He didn't do it either."

He pushed his fingers through his hair. "According to his mother Petey didn't get along with Susan. They argued a lot. There seemed to be a rivalry between them. Did he ever say anything to you?"

"No, and if you really think Petey killed Susan, then why would he call me?"

"It's possible he wanted to get caught or to have someone stop him," he said. "Hell, he might have wanted to frame you because of what you were doing with his sister."

I resisted the urge to tell Nash about my conversation with Edward McKinley. "A lot of brothers and sisters don't get along," I said, "but they don't kill one another."

He picked up a ruler from my desk and tapped it several times. "Petey's been under a lot of pressure trying to be the man of the house since his father left and his brother died," he said. "Teachers tell me he's been getting into trouble lately."

"His brother drowned five years ago," I said, "and his father's been gone for six. There's got to be another reason Petey's acting up."

He shrugged. "Maybe things just caught up with him. It's too much of a coincidence that the kid tells you to meet him where his sister ends up dead." He hesitated. "If that's what happened."

"It happened," I said.

"I tried to reach the woman you were with that night, but I haven't had any luck.

"She was away for a couple of days. She's back now."

He nodded. "Your friends tell me you're a real lady's man, Mr. Asher. You date a few teachers here at school, a woman who works in the cafeteria and a policewoman in town. Hell, you even still see your ex-wife. How do you keep them all happy?"

"Lieutenant, if you don't have any other questions, I'm going to eat my lunch, now."

"I've got to go anyway," he said. "Got a few more of Susan's friends to talk to. One of them claims to have seen her latest boyfriend."

I pointed my finger at him. "I'm not going to argue with you about my relationship with Susan."

"Fair enough," he said.

We left the classroom and walked down the corridor in silence. When we got to the top of the stairs, Nash said, "I just found out Susan kept a diary. Her mother's agreed to let me look at it. I'm on my way over there now." His eyes locked on mine as if studying my reaction.

"I hope it clears things up," I said, then turned and headed for the cafeteria. I vaguely remember a couple of students saying, "hi" to me as I entered. The police getting Susan's diary should have made me feel better, but it didn't. A woman capable of telling her friends lies could also write them in her diary.

The cafeteria workers looked at me strangely. Usually I stopped to talk. I bought a Coke and a bag of chips and went back to my room.

My last two classes dragged by. I had trouble concentrating. The students noticed my preoccupation and were quieter than normal.

At the end of the school day I usually wander down to the teachers' room and swap stories with other members of the faculty. Today I shut the door, sat at my desk and listened as the sounds of students laughing and slamming lockers gradually receded.

I tried to correct papers but got lost in thought. I remembered a time when I was eight years old. A teenage gang was smashing car windows in our neighborhood. Everyone knew who was doing it, but no one was willing to go to the police knowing that the kids wouldn't be punished and would quickly be back out on the streets. My father went to the cops. The gang members were arrested, and released. The windows on our house and car were broken. As a young boy I couldn't understand why my dad had gone to the police if he knew that was going to happen. He told me that justice was important and it sometimes needed all the help it could get. I hadn't thought about that incident in a long time.

I don't know how long I had been sitting there when there was a knock on the door. Rita Dooley walked in. The smile on her face looked out of place.

"I thought you'd want to know," she said. "I just heard it myself. Petey's been spotted. They're going to get him now."

CHAPTER 9

I smiled and for the first time all day really meant it. "That's great," I said. "Where?"

"Out in western Massachusetts," she said. "A town called Hadley."

"Interesting," I said. "The Olivers had a cottage, in Hadley, on the Connecticut River. Did you know that?"

She shook her head. "How could they afford a place on the river?"

"It wasn't much from the way Petey described it. An uncle left it to them when he died. Is that where they found him?"

"No. He was recognized by a grocery store owner who called the police and then tried to stall him. By the time the cops got there he was gone, but at least now we know where he is. It shouldn't take too long to pick him up."

"I wonder how he got way out there," I said.

Rita shrugged. "Maybe he had bus fare."

I thought about the money that Cynthia Oliver said he had taken. "What happens when the police pick him up?"

"They question him about Susan. If they're satisfied he wasn't involved he goes back to his family."

"So he can run away again?" I said.

"Steve, he belongs with his family."

"I know that," I said, "but before he goes back someone he trusts has to talk to him. He told me on the phone he found something. Whatever it was upset him. He may not be honest with the police. Let me talk to him. Find out what's wrong."

"It's not up to me. The Hadley cops will talk to him first. Then Nash will question him. He'll decide when to take Petey home."

"Can you talk to Nash?"

"Sure, but I don't know if it'll do any good." She put her hand on my shoulder. "I'll call you if I hear anything."

I checked my mailbox on my way out of school. A message said that Lisa Gerrault had called and would be at her office until four. Ten minutes later I was led in by her secretary. Lisa was a friend of Beth's and during our marriage I had seen a lot of her. She was never overly friendly to me. It was almost like she tolerated me because I was her friend's husband. She probably wasn't thrilled Beth and I were back together. Thing was, she was a good lawyer and when I felt I needed legal advice she was the first person I thought of.

Her office was a square room with a row of bookcases behind her sturdy-looking wooden desk. A picture of her husband and two children stood in front of a bank of law books. I noticed one of Beth's paintings on the wall.

"Impressive," I said looking around the office.

Lisa leaned back in her chair. She was Beth's age but the gray in her short brown hair made her look older. "Sorry I didn't get back to you sooner," she said motioning me to sit down. "I was away all weekend. Heard you had quite a scare on Friday."

"I think I might need a lawyer." I told her the whole story from Petey's phone call right up to being questioned by Nash at school and Susan having a diary. She was a good listener, not bothered by the phone lines buzzing in the background.

When I finished she said, "Damn right you need a lawyer. When you couldn't get me you should have called someone else."

"I kept thinking the police would make an arrest."

"You never talk to the cops without a lawyer present." She shook her head. "I can't believe you talked to Nash three times."

"How could I not talk to him, for God's sake. I found Susan's body."

"All the more reason. Did he read you your rights?"

"No. Why the hell would he do that? There's nothing linking me to Susan's death."

"You just happened to be the one who found her body."

"Right."

"Has Nash been asking people about you?"

I nodded. "He was at school today."

She leaned forward in her chair. "I'm sure he was. He's going to look at your school records and talk to everyone who knows you. Hell, he might even go through your trash."

I leaned forward. "He'll check to see if I have a police record, won't he?"

"Of course. Why, are you hiding something?"

I shook my head. Beth knew about what happened to Mitch and the subsequent investigation, but I didn't think she'd mentioned it to Lisa.

Lisa picked up a pen and tapped it. "From now on don't say anything unless you have a lawyer with you." She narrowed her eyes. "Will they find anything in Susan's diary about you?"

"Nothing."

She looked over my head and her eyes glazed. I wondered if Beth had confided in her about the times she thought I was cheating on her.

"Ed McKinley," she said. "I wonder what he has to do with all this?"

"According to him, nothing."

"Right. Mr. Clean."

"Can you help?" I said.

She drummed her fingers on her desk. "I haven't had anything to do with Criminal Law since I got out of law school. Let me see what I can find out. If I can't handle it I'll put you in contact with someone who can."

When I got back to my car I put my head back on the seat and closed my eyes. Talking to Lisa had made me feel worse. The police investigation won't find anything to tie me to Susan's murder. It was other things that Nash might turn up that troubled me. Maybe seeing Susan's diary will help them find the real killer and they'll leave me alone so I can teach my kids.

I decided to stop at Beth's on my way home. I wanted to tell her about my conversation with Lisa and that Petey had been seen. Maybe the cops had already picked him up.

Beth lived in a five-room brick ranch on the north side of the city. Her parents had lived in it. Three years ago they moved to up-state New York to be closer to their son and new grandchild. That's when Beth moved in.

Her Escort was in the yard. When she opened the door I could tell she was upset.

"What's wrong," I said.

"Did you see the afternoon Tribune?"

"No. Why?"

"It's on the coffee table."

"What's in it?"

"Read it," she said walking into the kitchen. "Then we'll talk."

I picked the paper up off the table. The story was on page one.

"Local teacher connected to Oliver case," the headline read. The byline was Aaron Fleming.

I sat down on the couch. A knot tightened in my stomach as I started to read.

"The Tribune has seen a copy of Susan Oliver's diary," it started. "It revealed a relationship with Steven Asher, a Social Studies teacher at North Middle School in Waltham. Asher has denied any personal relationship with the woman, but the diary contradicts his statements and lists dates and times they met.

"Susan describes Asher's lovemaking as 'kinky and bizarre,' and tells of his obsession to keep their relationship quiet, 'because the school committee wouldn't understand his love for me because I'm young and Petey is my brother.' She mentions a 'troubled relation-ship' Asher had with his ex-wife and describes a birthmark Asher has as being 'extremely erotic.'

"Eyewitnesses claim to have seen Asher and Oliver together out-side of school. In our exclusive interview with Asher about his dis-covery of Susan Oliver's body he made no mention of his involve-ment with the Oliver woman. Asher was unavailable for comment about the latest development.

"The police will not confirm that Asher is a suspect, but we have learned they questioned teachers at North Middle today about Asher, and a source close to the investigation has said that Asher is a prime suspect in the murder. The autopsy performed on Susan's body indicates she was pregnant."

The rest of the story told of the murder and discovery of the body. My hands shook as I reread the first part of the story.

"It's bullshit," I said heading toward the kitchen. "All of it."

Beth leaned against the counter. "Why would Susan lie in her diary?"

"I don't know." I banged my fist on the table. "That son of a bitch Fleming. How could that bastard print those lies? I should go over to the Tribune and throw his computer out the window and him right after it."

"Probably make you feel better, but it wouldn't accomplish anything. How did Susan know about your birthmark?"

"I don't know. It's ridiculous. Would you describe my lovemaking as kinky and bizarre?"

"Not with me."

"Not with anyone."

"The story made it sound like the police are ready to arrest you."

I ran my fingers through my hair and glanced toward the kitchen window. "She made up a fantasy. I don't know why." I hesitated. "You know I didn't kill her."

"That's not even a question. It's what the police are going to do that worries me."

"Tell me about it. Fleming's article said she gave dates and times we met. It shouldn't be too hard to prove I wasn't with her."

"It wouldn't be difficult for Susan to find out what nights you were home," Beth said. "Your car would've been in the yard. She could've made up her stories about those nights."

I thought about what McKinley said about Susan stalking him, and then I thought about the two break-ins at my apartment earlier in the year. "I'm gonna call Fleming."

I dialed his number at the Trib. "You bastard," I said when he got on the line. "I should come over there and beat the shit out of you."

"Calm down, for Chrissake. The Globe and Herald will be running the story. I wanted to get there first."

"I can't believe you'd print that garbage. None of it's true. It's irresponsible reporting and the Trib is going to have a lawsuit on its hands."

"It's all in Susan's diary. I just wrote what people would want to know. I ran it by my editor. You wanna sue, go ahead. It'll make for a great story."

"How'd you get the diary?"

"That's none of your business."

"The hell it's not. Cynthia Oliver, right? What'd you do, pay her to let you look at it?"

"You know I can't reveal my source. What'd you want me to do, sit on the story? I did what I thought was right. You do believe in the First Amendment, don't you?"

"What I believe in is fair and accurate reporting. You could have gotten my side and put that in the story."

"I called you at school and left a message. Didn't you get it?"

"I got it."

"I had a ten o'clock deadline so I went with what I had. You said you never dated her. Everything in that story has been verified. You want your side presented, give me an interview. I'll print it tomorrow."

"Fuck you."

He hung up.

I slammed Beth's wall phone so hard I thought I might have cracked the plastic.

I don't know how long I was thinking before I became aware Beth was staring at me. "What are you going to do?" she said.

"First thing I'm going to do is talk to Lisa about suing the Tribune for slander." I told Beth about going to Lisa's office.

"First thing you're going to do is sit down." She pointed to a chair. "Fleming wouldn't have printed it if it wasn't in Susan's diary. Wouldn't do any good to go after the Trib."

I sat down. "Twenty years ago I thought that lies were going to ruin my life. Now it's happening again."

"I know, honey. This time you can't just sit back."

I got up and began to pace. My breathing slowly returned to normal. "You're right. I've got to prove that everything in Susan's diary about me is a lie."

"That's a good place to start."

I nodded, then smiled. "I came over to tell you that the cops spotted Petey out in Hadley. They were on their way to get him. I gotta get home. I told Rita I'd wait for her call."

Beth's body stiffened. "Wouldn't want to disappoint Rita."

"Wait a minute. That's not fair. Rita and I haven't dated since you and I started or is there something else going on here?" I paused. "You do believe I wasn't dating Susan don't you?"

She smiled, but it looked forced. "Yeah, I do. I'm just worried about you that's all."

"I'm worried too. This is scaring the shit out of me."

CHAPTER 10

There were no messages on my machine when I arrived home. I corrected a few papers, but couldn't concentrate. Richard cooed, cackled and whistled while I tried to watch television. Oprah was doing a show on child abuse. I switched it off and tried to read a book. It didn't work. My mind kept drifting and I'd stare at the phone as if willing Rita to call.

I went to the refrigerator for a Coke. I drank and paced the floor. My students were going to read that garbage in the Tribune. Hell, everybody was going to read it. It pissed me off that Susan's lies were front page news. The cops would probably believe them. And what about Beth? If she was having doubts about our relationship the rumors weren't going to help.

I had to find out why Susan lied about me and prove it wasn't true.

When the phone rang I picked it up on the first ring.

"Steve Asher," a male voice said.

"Speaking."

"This is Darrell Jenkins from the Boston Globe," he said. "Do you have any comment to make about the information found in Susan Oliver's diary?"

"None," I said. "No. Wait a minute. I never had a relationship with Susan. What she wrote was a fantasy."

"What about the birthmark?"

"She must have talked to someone."

"But certainly...."

"That's all I've got to say."

After I hung up I thought about how what I said would be used in the paper. Maybe it would have been smarter to tell my side. I ran things through my mind. Maybe I should call Nash and take the offensive. I couldn't do that yet. I needed proof that I didn't date Susan.

At nine-thirty the doorbell rang. It was Rita.

"Nothing on Petey," she said. I could see the frustration in her eyes.

She walked upstairs and sat on the couch. I got her a Coke out of the refrigerator then sat beside her.

"The Hadley police are going to search all night and they've called in more people to look tomorrow. Someone claims to have spotted him in Northampton. It's just a matter of time before they pick him up."

"Did you talk to Nash about me seeing Petey?"

"Yeah. He said he'd wait and see how things went. I tried to convince him you could be helpful. Don't think it worked."

"At least Petey can tell him he called me and that's why I was at Walden. Maybe he saw something."

"Maybe he saw who killed Susan and that's why he ran off." She hesitated. "I read the story in the Tribune."

"I wasn't dating Susan."

"I didn't think so. Keeping it a secret wouldn't be your style." She put her hand on my shoulder. "If you need someone to talk to, I'm here."

"Thanks. Did Nash mention the diary?"

She shook her head. "Just said he wants to talk to you."

"I bet he does. I talked to Lisa Gerrault today. She told me not to talk to the cops unless I had a lawyer present."

"Does that include me?"

I smiled. "I didn't know you were a cop."

"What's Beth's take on all this?"

"She believes me."

Our eyes locked for a few seconds. Then she turned away and took a sip of her Coke. "I gotta go," she said. "I'll call you if I hear anything."

I listened as Rita's car started and she pulled away from the house. I felt an attraction to her and after my talk with Beth this afternoon I felt guilty. I turned on television, but had trouble focusing. "Petey, why are you still running?" I said aloud. At eleven when the phone rang I pounced on it.

"Steve, this is Jim Stafford."

I hesitated. The superintendent of schools hadn't called me at home in a long time.

"Sorry to call you this late, but I just got out of a meeting." He paused. "I don't like what I'm hearing about you and the Oliver woman. What the hell's going on?"

"None of it's true."

"Are you saying she lied in her own diary?"

"Yeah. I wish I knew why."

He hesitated for a few seconds. "I've known you for twelve years, Steve. Christ, I hired you and I'm usually a pretty good judge of character. Whether you're involved in the woman's death or not, your name keeps coming up. The school committee doesn't like it and, quite frankly, neither do I."

"It's going to take the cops some time to find out the truth."

"I know, but meanwhile parents have been calling. A couple of members of the committee want me to suspend you pending the results of the investigation."

"They can't do that. Hell, I was the union representative for ten years. I know my rights. I haven't been convicted of anything."

"They can suspend you with pay until we see what happens. We've done it before."

"I had nothing to do with Susan's murder."

"Steve, take some personal time. A few days. Maybe the police will make an arrest by then."

"Taking time off makes it look like I've got something to hide. I won't do that."

"How do you think your students are going to react reading about their teacher in the paper like that?"

"I'll just tell them the truth. Don't underestimate them. They can tell when someone's lying to them." I paused. "I'm innocent, but my whole career could be destroyed by heresay. Doesn't the committee want to wait for the truth?"

"Steve, I'm trying to buy you some time. I know how it'll look if we suspend you."

"I understand that, but put yourself in my place." I struggled to keep my voice under control. "What would you do if the school committee was thinking about suspending you for something you had no involvement in? Sit back and say okay. I don't think so. I think you'd fight it. Hell, I teach my kids it's wrong to turn away when they see an injustice. This one is being done to me and I'm not running away from it."

"It's with pay, for chrissake. It'll be like a vacation."

"I've worked for you a long time, Jim, but obviously you don't know me very well. I think you've already made up your mind. It doesn't matter what I say, does it?"

"I wish there was some other way I could handle this. Look, take tomorrow off. I'll talk to the committee. See if I can put them off for a few days, but I want you to think about taking some personal time."

"It wouldn't do me any good to argue, would it?"

"I've made my decision. It's the best thing for everyone. The committee could suspend you indefinitely. I don't want that to happen."

"I appreciate it, Jim."

He hung up.

I sat for a few seconds, then banged my fist on the couch. The superintendent's words circled in my mind. The past twelve years of my life had revolved around kids. When I read the paper or watched television I'd think about how I could take the information and turn it into a relevant lesson for them. It's what I've wanted to do since I was a kid. Even during the summer I took courses to get ready for the next year. I realized that as long as the police considered me a suspect there was a chance the school committee wouldn't let me teach. I shook my head. And besides that, Nash was digging into my past and there was no way I could stop him.

I tried to sleep, but kept tossing and turning. At five I got up, took a shower and by six-thirty I was finishing my third cup of coffee. I looked at the wall clock. Then I called Rita Dooley.

She answered on the first ring. I could tell by her voice that she hadn't gotten much sleep either. Petey hadn't been found. More people were going to be mobilized in Hadley.

I poured another cup of coffee and thought about what I wanted to do. Then I fed Richard and by seven I was on the road. Hadley was a two-hour trip from Waltham. I pulled onto Route 2, put The Temptations on the tape deck and stepped on the gas.

When I looked at the speedometer, I was doing seventy. I checked my mirror for cops and pressed harder on the gas. I wanted to be there if the police brought Petey in.

I drove along the Mohawk Trail and exited Route 202. My grandmother had lived in Holyoke, a city not far from Hadley. My family had driven this route many times when I was a kid. Then, Hadley was just a road sign to me. The place that you went through just before you crossed the Connecticut River. I tried to remember what it was like.

Twenty-five years ago large tracts of farmland bordered both sides of the road leading into town. Today as I whizzed past fast food restaurants and shopping malls I realized how much things had changed. I got directions to the police station and stopped to ask about joining the search. The cop on duty told me they were focusing on the Northampton side of the river, but they didn't want any civilian volunteers at this point.

I continued driving. It was close to nine when I took a left onto a dirt road which ran along the Hadley side of the river. A large field of high grass was on my left and cottages lined the river on my right. Most seemed run-down and deserted. Some were boarded up as if getting ready for a rough winter, but a few looked like people lived in them year-round. The Oliver cottage had to be on this road.

I drove slowly looking for a cruiser. The cops would probably have some men at the cabin, but when I got to the end of the long, winding road I hadn't spotted one. I circled back and asked an old man walking along the road for directions.

He leaned down and squinted. "You helpin' out with the search?"

I nodded.

"Won't do you any good to look at the cottage. The police were all over it yesterday. Ain't no one there today."

"I want to give it a quick check," I said. "Just in case the kid comes back."

"Suit yourself," he said, "but you want my opinion, if the kid doesn't want to be found there's plenty of places for him to hide. If he's smart he could hold up for months."

The driveway to the Olivers was about five hundred feet long with hard, rutted earth which became flattened and more worn down as I got closer to the cabin.

The cottage was a gray slate box-like structure with a chimney on one side. Oak and pine trees were clumped along the side, separating it from its nearest neighbor. The ground sloped downward toward the river. Tire marks crisscrossed the dirt, and the surrounding grassland was beaten down as if it had been trampled.

I got out of the car and zipped up my jacket. It was sunny, but the wind off the water felt cold against my skin. The two closest cabins were boarded up. In the distance, on the other side of a cornfield I could see another cabin. A green Volkswagon van was parked in front.

At the Olivers a screened in porch faced the water. I tried the door. It was locked. I gazed down a steep embankment which led to the river.

I walked around the cabin. Two oversized windows were on each side of the house with two smaller ones in back. Thick black curtains made it difficult to look inside, but one curtain was parted. I peered in to see that most of the furniture was covered with beige drop clothes. A large gray chair rested against a wall covered with barnboard. It didn't look like anyone had been inside for awhile.

A bulkhead led to a basement door. I jumped down the steps and tried to look inside. The windows were caked with dirt. I spit on my finger and tried to wipe it clean. Then I noticed that the lock had been broken. I opened the door and gazed inside. In the darkness I could make out an empty coal bin. I squinted. Furniture covered with drop clothes seemed to fill every inch. I stepped inside and listened. Nothing. I shut the door and left.

I circled the cabin one more time, then started across the cornfield in the direction of the Volkswagon. If Petey were around I wanted him to see me.

The other cottage was built like Petey's only smaller. I looked back across the field. There was a clear view of the Olivers' place.

The door to the cottage opened and a man walked down the steps. He appeared to be in his early fifties. He wore a denim shirt, brown chinos and work boots. His long gray hair was tied back into a pony tail.

"You people just won't give up, will ya?" he said.

"Were there a lot of people around yesterday?" I said.

He squinted. "Yeah and they did a lot of damage tramping

through the field. The kid's not around."

"I'm his teacher," I said. "If Petey is around and sees someone he knows he may come out."

"His teacher. That's really touching," he said. "If you want to really help him, leave him be. He'll come in when he's ready."

"Petey's only thirteen."

"Shit, I ran away from home when I was twelve. I had my reasons. So does the kid."

I stared at him. "Would you help him if he came to you? Maybe hide him out."

"Cops asked me the same question. Said they wanted to question him in connection with his sister's murder. I don't need that kind of shit. Last thing I want is trouble with the cops again."

"Have you seen anyone at the Oliver place recently?" I said.

"Just them fags from Northampton," he said. "Them and their loud parties. Hey, live and let live I always say."

"How do you know they're gay,"

"I could tell by lookin' at em, just like I can tell that you're straight."

"Did you live here when the Olivers used to come?"

He nodded. "Yeah. I was here when the kid drowned, too. He was living there with his old man. Went out in a rowboat and fell overboard. He was queer, too."

"You could tell by looking at him," I said.

"Right. I hadn't seen the Olivers in so long I thought they sold the place till the cops told me different. You want to look around, you stay off my property."

He narrowed his eyes and watched me. I resisted the urge to blow him a kiss and slowly headed across the field back to the Olivers. This might have been a waste of time, but I wasn't ready to give up yet.

I circled the cabin one more time and was about to walk up to the main road and have a look in the field when I heard a faint tap as if someone had closed a door. I doubled back and rechecked the place. This time I noticed that the basement door was slightly ajar. I had closed it after I checked it earlier. Maybe Petey was hiding there.

I jumped down the steps, pulled the door open and gazed inside.

"Petey," I said.

Silence.

I went to my car, returned with my flashlight and flipped it on. The floor was caked with dirt. Footsteps were clearly visible. I moved in a few steps and ducked to avoid hitting a heating pipe. Ahead I saw a furnace built of cast iron which looked like it would last forever.

I hesitated. Maybe the wind had blown the door open. There didn't seem to be anyone in the basement. I wasn't afraid of the dark, but of rats that might feel this place belonged to them. I took one more look around and was about to go out into the sunlight when I heard a low shuffling sound like a foot sliding across the floor.

The sound came from behind me. I started to turn toward it, but before I could I heard a sharp intake of breath and felt a solid blow to the back of my head. I put my hand up to protect myself. I was hit again, this time so hard I could feel myself falling.

CHAPTER 11

My head thudded on the cement floor. My vision blurred, but I didn't pass out. I heard heavy breathing and footsteps moving quickly up the steps. I blinked several times. In the sunlight I could see black shoes disappearing onto the grass.

The footsteps moved away from the cottage and gradually faded. I pushed myself up, resting my back against the furnace. I shook my head, trying to clear it.

I felt a small lump on the back of my head. I stood up straight for a few seconds, then slowly walked outside. The sun hurt my eyes and I coughed from the dust I had inhaled. I shielded my eyes and looked toward the road. No one was around.

The green Volkswagon was still parked in the driveway across the field. The neighbor had worn brown work boots. Whoever hit me had on black shoes. That ruled Petey out too. Petey always wore high tops.

A car accelerated out on the road. I sprinted toward the driveway, but the car had disappeared. Whoever had hit me could have killed me. I wondered why they didn't. I leaned against my car. My head hurt and thoughts circled in my brain. Petey's phone call. Finding Susan's body. Her diary, the break-ins and now being attacked. Thing was, I wasn't feeling fear, only anger.

I went back to the cellar, picked up my light and flipped it on. I remembered the last time I had used it. The night I found Susan's body.

The basement was deserted, but in one corner the dirt was flattened as if someone had lain on the floor. I flashed the light toward the furnace. A crumpled Juicy Fruit gum wrapper lay behind it.

That was the kind of gum Petey chewed.

I went back to the car. The pain in my head turned to a dull throb as I drove back out to the main road. I checked my rearview mirror. There were no cars in sight. I'd have to be more careful.

I tried to think like Petey. If I were a kid trying to hide, where would I go, what would I do?

I rejected going to the police station and reporting the attack. Whoever did it was gone and going to the cops would waste time. I wanted the daylight hours to look for Petey.

On the other side of the river I saw two police cars parked beside some trees. A cop was leaning against one and smoking a cigarette. Another man walked along the shore, and I could see several people in the distance. At least I knew Petey hadn't been found yet.

I spent the next few hours searching around Northampton. Rita had said Petey had been spotted there. As the afternoon progressed I became more discouraged. I started to recognize places I'd already checked. When I stopped at a store to buy a Coke there were only a couple more hours of sunlight.

I sat on a bench in front of the store and stared at a park across the street. I pressed the cold bottle against the lump on the back of my head. I should just go home. Maybe Petey would call again.

Conversations I had with him flashed through my mind. He was an open kid who talked about his family as if testing me. His father's physical abuse of him and his sisters before the old man left, his mother's drinking and locking herself in her room until her husband calmed down. Most of all he talked about his fear that he may never get out of his neighborhood. That he may never amount to anything.

If Petey had left Northampton and headed west he'd cross the New York border. I thought of the towns in between and then I thought of The Summit. It was an amusement park on the top of a hill near here. Easy walking distance for a kid. Petey had mentioned it several times to me. He'd had good times there. Petey had run away three times before. I remembered him telling me he always went to places he knew. That's probably why he went to the family cabin. The more I thought about it, the more convinced I became that he'd be at The Summit.

I brought the bottle back inside, got directions from the storekeeper, then bought a ham and cheese sandwich and another Coke. I munched on my sandwich as I drove. Ten minutes later I passed a large sign telling me that The Summit, "The world's greatest small amusement park," was the next right.

The road leading up to it was steep and narrow and wound through a forest of maples and pine.

About a mile up I came to a wooden barricade. "Closed for the Season," "No Trespassing" and "Violators Subject to Arrest" was stenciled across the wooden frame.

I grabbed my flashlight, then got out of the car and opened my trunk. I needed something that would help me get inside the park. If I had thought this out I could have stopped at a hardware store and bought some wire cutters. All I had was a tire iron.

I checked the sky, then started to jog. There wasn't much sunlight left.

The incline grew steeper as I moved up the road. My legs started to ache. Crows cawed overhead and there were rustles in the trees as if small animals were in the woods.

Then the road started to level off and I saw the park. The roller coaster and ferris wheel hovered over it. As I got closer I saw the frames of game booths and penny arcades. A large sign on top of the entrance told me I had reached The Summit.

A chain link fence surrounded the park. Thick padlocks and heavy chains locked the gate. The game booths were boarded up, the miniature golf course was covered with leaves, the arcades were chained shut and padlocked.

I put my hand on the fence and peered inside. "Petey," I yelled. "It's Mr. Asher." My voice echoed in the stillness.

The fence around the park was about twenty feet high. I couldn't climb it without cutting myself on the barbed wire above it. I tried to pry it up with the tire iron, but it wouldn't budge.

Wisps of clouds floated overhead. I could see iridescent shades of pink in the sky and estimated that I had about thirty minutes of daylight left.

Huge boulders towered over the rear of the park. I walked toward them.

The sound of a car engine in the distance stopped me. It was faint at first. I held my breath, listening. In the stillness it was hard to pinpoint where it was coming from. It grew louder, then seemed to level off. It continued for about thirty seconds then cut out.

The sound seemed to have startled the birds. I listened a moment longer and heard nothing. Maybe it was the police on a routine patrol. I could explain what I was doing to them. If it was the person who attacked me at the cottage I had a problem. I quickened my pace.

The rocks extended about thirty feet into the air. Three of them piled one on top of the other as if someone had placed them that way. A few jagged edges jutted out and breaks in a half dozen places made it look easy to climb.

The boulders ran along the entire back side of the park and fell at a steep angle leaving a few feet of space between them and the fence.

I looked toward the road. No one was coming. If it was the cops they could have unlocked the gate and been here by now. The longer I didn't see anyone the more nervous I felt.

"Petey," I yelled again. If he was here why wouldn't he answer? Maybe he was afraid or maybe he didn't want me to find him.

I reached up and wrapped the iron over a rock edge, then put my foot in a crevice and pulled my body up. It gave slightly like it was eroded. Several stones fell around me and to the ground. Within minutes I was at the top.

I scampered across the rocks a few feet, then dropped down into the space behind the fence. It was like an alley, barely wide enough for me to fit, running the entire length of the park. I moved quickly along. A section of the fence was bent up and loose. I wrapped the tire iron around it and tugged. It groaned and twisted up. I got on the ground and rolled under.

I was behind the funhouse. To my left were the game booths. I moved around them and onto a cement path. It looped the park in a wide arcing circle.

The sun had fallen behind the trees. About fifteen minutes of light was left. "Petey," I yelled. No response. "Damn it," I said aloud and started to move quickly around the path.

One by one, I checked the game booths and rides. Then I examined the roller coaster, tilt-a-whirl, bumper cars and ferris wheel. I was torn between doing a careful check and covering the whole park while I still had some light.

The squeaking of my sneakers was the only sound in the quiet. I reached the entrance, squinted and stared toward the road. No one was coming.

I started to jog, hoping to cover the other side of the park quickly. The pain in my head, which had become an intermittent throbbing, began to ache again.

When I got back to the funhouse the darkness had settled in and I felt discouraged. I sat on a bench and rested the tire iron beside me. Maybe the car I heard was parked near mine, the person waiting for my return. A knot formed in my stomach.

I banged my fist against the bench, then got up and walked toward the back fence. I bent it upwards, then took one more look toward the park entrance. A light reflected off the trees in the distance. It was faint at first. It snapped off as if the person suddenly realized they were close to the park. I squinted and tried to make out what was happening. Through the darkness I couldn't see anything.

I moved back to the funhouse, tightened my grip on the tire iron and began to search for a place to hide. A thick padlock hung from the door. I moved to the rear of the building and pushed against the wall.

I heard footsteps, faint at first, but becoming louder as they approached the park. I flicked my flash on and off quickly to get my bearings. A huge storage chest, large enough to hold me, was against the side of the building. It wasn't locked.

I lifted the lid, straddled my leg over and began to move inside. I heard a sharp intake of breath, then a hand gripped my leg and shoved up causing me to lose my balance. The flashlight flew out of my hand and I toppled over landing on my back.

A figure scrambled out of the chest. "Shit," he said, then he began to sprint. It was Petey. He raced across the park toward the entrance.

CHAPTER 12

I jumped to my feet. Petey's footsteps thumped across the pavement. In the darkness I couldn't see in what direction he had gone.

"Petey, get down," I whispered as loud as I dared. "Someone's coming." I raced around to the front of the funhouse and out into the walkway just as a beam of light flashed into the park.

I pushed my back against the building and quickly moved to the rear. The lid to the storage chest was up. I reached over and put it down. Then I picked up the tire iron and listened.

At first I didn't hear anything. The wind had died down and the trees weren't moving. A pale moon was just visible behind the clouds. Suddenly the fence shook and I heard the muffled sound of a human voice.

I looked toward the rocks behind the park and felt an urge to run, get under the fence and up into the trees. If I was scared I could only imagine the terror Petey must be feeling. I couldn't run. I had to find him. Tell him everything was going to be all right. That I had a plan. I heard the wheeze of someone breathing heavily, then the fence shook violently again.

I put my hands on the edge of the building and stuck my head around the side. Near the entrance of the park I saw the glare of the flashlight. It swung and bobbed as he walked. The light illuminated him from the waist down. Two legs in step, moving toward the rocks. I noticed black shoes stride through the darkness along the chain-link fence.

A plan started to form in my mind. If I could get to the fence as he started to slide under I could hit him with the tire iron.

His light flashed on the boulders, then down the narrow alley behind the park between the fence and the rocks. The man groaned as if in frustration.

Nothing happened for several seconds. I took a few steps toward the fence. I had to time it perfectly. He must have turned, or maybe he heard something, because the light flashed toward me, almost catching me in its beam. I moved back against the building.

Light footsteps tapped along the parking lot, heading back toward the entrance. I let out a long breath and my shoulders relaxed. For an instant I thought he might be leaving.

Then I heard a click as if someone had cocked a gun. The explosion was deafening. The gunshot echoed in the hills and died away. I fell to the ground covering my head. I stayed that way for a few seconds, then lifted my head.

The shot seemed wild, more an attempt to get us to reveal ourselves then to hit anything.

But what if he'd been shooting at Petey.

I forced myself to get up. I gripped the tire iron and moved a few feet to the side of a game booth. The soft sucking sounds my sneakers made seemed loud in the quiet.

A miniature golf course circled the center of the park. I remembered a small fence with two horizontal wooden poles surrounding it. I moved forward in the darkness until my hand struck the fence. Then I climbed over it, slid behind a tree and listened.

Off to my right I heard a sharp intake of breath.

"Petey?" I whispered.

No response.

I was afraid to move from the shelter of the tree. "It's Mr. Asher."

Still no response.

I looked toward the park entrance, then crouched down. "For Chrissake, I know you're here. What's wrong with you?"

Footsteps pounded on the pavement going away from me. A figure sprinted down the path. I raced after him, grabbed Petey by the shoulder and pushed him against the side of a building.

He pulled away. "Damn it. Leave me alone."

I pointed my finger at him. "Look, I don't know why you're trying to get away from me, but that guy out there isn't playing games. Maybe we can get out of this if we work together."

He took several short, quick breaths, then his shoulders relaxed and he nodded.

I tilted my head and listened, then motioned him back to the funhouse.

When we got there Petey said, "He's gone."

"I don't think so."

He pushed back the brim of his Red Sox cap. He was only a few inches away, but in the moonlight I could barely see his face.

"I heard him walk toward the road right after the shot."

"That's what he probably wants us to think. He's still out there."

Petey walked to the storage chest, pulled something out and put it on the ground beside me. It was his backpack. Then he sat down and rested his head against the building. He was breathing deeply.

"You want to tell me what's going on with you?" I stood over him trying to keep the anger out of my voice.

He turned away. "What the hell was that guy shooting at?" he said.

"Probably trying to flush us out. Right now he's not really sure we're inside. Unless we do something stupid we got some time to figure out how to get out of this. He can't see us in the dark and if he turns on his light we'll know where he is." I stared at him for a few seconds. "You okay?"

"Yeah," he said softly. "How did you find me?"

"I figured you'd go someplace familiar." I bent down and zipped up his jacket. "You must be hungry."

He shook his head. "I ate."

I sat down beside him. I could feel the tension in his body. We stayed that way for a few minutes.

"I'm sorry about Susan," I said.

He looked away.

I put my hand on his shoulder and waited a few seconds. "Did you see it happen?"

He shook his head. "But I'm responsible."

I expected him to say more. When he didn't, I said, "You can't blame yourself for what happened."

"If I didn't run away, she wouldn't have come looking for me. I just couldn't stay in that house anymore." He hesitated. "I'm not going back. No one's gonna make me."

"Look, Petey, Susan's dead. Right now you have a responsibility to your family. They need you. When you're eighteen, you can leave home. It's something to look forward to."

"Don't treat me like a kid. I know what I'm doing. They don't care about me."

"I can't imagine what you're going through. But you can't run away all the time."

We sat in silence for several minutes. I could feel him start to relax. Then he said, "You really have a parakeet?"

I had told Petey about Richard once at school.

"A guy doesn't lie about something like that. I named him after Little Richard."

"The guy who does impressions?" Petey said.

"No, that's Rich Little. Little Richard is the king of rock n' roll."

"Back in the old days," Petey said.

I smiled. "Watch it or I'll start to sing 'Tutti Frutti'."

"Probably scare the guy away," he said.

Petey put his head back against the building. "How we gonna get out of here?"

"We'll find a way," I said.

He nodded and closed his eyes.

"Petey, I have to ask you some things about Susan."

"Okay."

"How'd she know you were at Walden?"

He pulled the collar of his jacket up. "I called the house. Wanted them to know I was all right and why I wasn't coming home. Susan answered the phone. She knew I went to Walden sometimes to think. She must have figured it out."

"So how'd your medallion end up at the murder scene?"

He didn't answer for several seconds, then shrugged. "I haven't seen it for awhile."

"The police are going to ask you about it," I said.

He jumped to his feet. "I gotta get out of here."

I got up and grabbed his arm. "Not now. We'll wait for awhile, but when we do get out, you're going home."

He pulled his arm away. "No fuckin' way."

"You were hiding from me, weren't you? You figured I'd make you go home. Well, you're right."

He let out a long breath.

"I'll be right with you," I said. "I found Susan's body. The police consider me a suspect. It's important that you tell them everything you know. You got to trust me on this."

He sat back down.

"There was a story in the Tribune saying Susan and I dated."

"I know," he said. "She told me you two were going out. Said you wanted to keep it quiet and I shouldn't mention it 'cause it might embarrass you. I thought it was cool."

"It wasn't true. I never dated Susan. Any idea why she'd lie?"

He shrugged. "Susan acted strange sometimes. She was always arguing with Mom about things."

"What kind of things?"

He stared into the darkness, then reached into his pants pocket, pulled out a package of cigarettes and slid one out. I reached over to take it from him. He pulled away and lit it with a lighter. The flame shot up in the darkness.

"Put it out," I said.

He took a deep puff. "I've been smoking since I was ten. Other kids do drugs. Not me."

The shot was so loud it seemed to shake the buildings. The bullet ricocheted off the path near us. I threw myself over Petey and ducked my head waiting for another shot. Petey wrapped his arms around me and was breathing heavily. The light from a flash was sweeping the walkway. Then it went off.

"Let's go," I said. I grabbed Petey's hand and sprinted along the back fence. I didn't know where I was running to. I just wanted to get away. I stopped and pressed against the back of a building. Maybe we could get under the fence and over the rocks before he got a clear shot at us. I looked at Petey. I couldn't take the chance.

"Why'd he shut off the light," Petey said.

"He doesn't want us to know exactly where he is. That way he can surprise us."

Petey nodded. He seemed calmer than I was.

"There's a worn down part of the rocks over there." He pointed toward the fence. "It's almost like a path leading up into the woods. I slid under the fence in front of it. Maybe we could get out that way."

"Let's sit tight. See if we can get a sense of where the guy is."

Ten minutes must have gone by. The sound didn't register at first, just the slight rustle of a branch. Then I heard a rock thump on the pavement. The guy was climbing the rocks. In a few seconds he'd be in the alley.

"Think you can find that path in the dark?"

Petey nodded.

When I heard the thud of shoes on the pavement and the groan of the fence I knew the guy had found where I got in. I waited a few seconds then whispered, "Now."

Petey scampered toward the fence, rolled under, then held it up for me. We raced across the alley, through the rock crevice and fell to our stomachs as we reached the top. The light flashed toward us just as we ducked down. It stayed on for a few seconds, then went out.

The fence creaked. I could envision the man crawling back out into the alley. It would take a few seconds for him to find the path. I motioned to Petey and we raced toward the woods. Trees rustled and branches snapped as we ran. The vegetation got thicker as we moved. After a few minutes we stopped. "Let's head toward the main road, but stay in the trees," I said. "Guy's gonna have to use his light if he wants to find us. If we see it, you take off. I'll catch up with you."

I stared in the direction of the park and wondered what made this guy so intent on getting us. There had to be something Petey wasn't telling me.

I was about to ask him when a noise in the distance caught my attention. It was low, but unmistakable. A police siren. It grew louder. Petey stopped and his body tensed.

I grabbed his shoulder just as he tried to run. "The guy's still around. We've got to go to the cops. Tell them what happened. They can get him."

The sirens grew louder, almost deafening in the stillness. Brakes squealed and gravel hit the side of the cars. We saw lights in the distance.

Petey slapped my hand off his shoulder. "You led them here. If it wasn't for you they never would have found me." He began to run.

I moved after him, but he was quicker than I was. "Susan's dead," I said. "Whatever you think of your family, your place is with them."

Trees rustled and his footsteps began to fade. In the darkness I couldn't tell which direction he had gone.

"Damn it," I yelled. "I'm going to keep looking for you and the next time you won't get away. I care about what happens to you. The cops will take you home. You'll be safe."

For an instant there was silence. Then I heard his footsteps again, this time moving toward me.

He came through the trees and stood inches away from me. I could barely see him. He reached inside his backpack, pulled something out and handed it to me. It was a small brown bag. "This is what I found. Before you do anything, look at it. Then do what you think is best. Okay?"

"What is it?"

"You gotta promise me?" he said.

I heard doors slam and the sound of voices in the distance. I nodded and tucked the bag inside my jacket. Then we walked out of the woods and went to talk to the cops.

CHAPTER 13

Headlights from two cruisers illuminated the lot. Four policemen with flashlights were standing in front of the park entrance. One spotted us and motioned to the others. They walked in our direction.

Petey's eyes darted right and left as if searching for a way to escape. Then he tucked his hands into his pockets and we walked quickly toward the policemen.

Two officers stayed back while the other two approached us. One put his hand to his gun.

"A guy took a shot at us." I pointed toward the road. "He couldn't have gotten very far. If you hurry you can get him."

One of the cops looked toward the road, then headed back to the cruiser. He whispered something to the other two.

"Is that right, son?" the other cop said.

Petey nodded.

"It's Petey Oliver," I said. "I'm Steve Asher, his teacher. For chrissake the guy's getting away."

The officer flashed his light at us. "It's the Oliver kid, all right," he yelled to the others. "Is he your teacher?"

"Yeah."

The three cops got into the cruiser and sped away down the road.

The cop who approached us was tall and lanky. He appeared to be in his fifties. He smiled and put his hands on Petey's shoulder. "Are you all right?" When Petey didn't answer he looked at me.

I shrugged.

"There's only one car by the fence. That yours?"

I nodded, then remembered how long it took the man to walk up to the park. "The guy must have parked out on the highway."

"You sure it was a man?"

"Pretty sure," I said.

"If he's still around we'll get him." The cop refocused on Petey. "A lot of people are going to be real happy you're safe. Any idea who was shooting at you?"

Petey pushed his hands deeper into his pockets and stared off at the trees.

"Why don't you tell him what you know?" I said.

Petey narrowed his eyes.

I stared at him and our eyes locked. Then I refocused on the cop. "He thinks you wouldn't have found him if it wasn't for me. Whoever shot at us followed me figuring I'd lead him to Petey. I don't know why. I think Petey does. It's important that he gets protection until the guy's picked up."

"Anything you want to tell us, Petey?" the cop said.

Petey ignored the question and stared toward the trees.

I put my hand on his shoulder. He knocked it off with his hand and pulled away.

"First thing we gotta do is get young Mr. Oliver to the station. Then we'll talk."

He walked Petey to the cruiser, opened the back door and Petey climbed in. Then he turned to me. "You should have called us if you knew where the kid was."

"I wasn't really sure. I was at the Oliver place earlier today and somebody attacked me. It must have been the guy who shot at us." I explained what had happened. "No one knew I was coming out here, but someone followed me."

"Sure seems that way."

"Look, I know Petey pretty well. He knows something about this."

The cop shut the door of the cruiser and moved toward the driver's side. "Motel owner down on the highway reported seeing cars driving up here. Then he heard shots. Come on. I'll give you a lift to your car. Gonna want you to come down to the station and make a statement."

"You okay, Petey?" I said as I slid into the cruiser

He looked out the window and didn't respond.

The cop dropped me at my car, pulled in front and waited. I slipped the brown bag out of my jacket and emptied a video cassette on the seat beside me. The outside package said Memorex. My mind flashed to the break-in. Whoever trashed my apartment must have been looking for this.

Withholding evidence from the police is not something I ever thought I would do, but I promised Petey I'd look at it. A few hours shouldn't make much difference. Whatever was on it had upset him. Maybe once I knew what it was I could convince him to talk. Then I'd turn it over to Nash.

They put me in an office at the station and I gave a statement. Then I sat on a bench near the front entrance and waited for Petey. The woman behind the desk brought me a mug of coffee. I wrapped my hand around it and sipped. It was close to midnight when Petey came down the hallway with cops on either side of him. His head was down and the brim of his baseball cap almost covered his eyes. He had his hands shoved inside his denim jacket pockets.

"You all right?" I said as he walked past me. He didn't look up.

I followed them out the door of the station. "Petey, I'm going home with you. If you want me to come in I will."

A cop opened the back door of the cruiser and Petey slid in.

"Any sign of the guy who shot at us?" I said to the cop.

He shook his head.

"Petey doesn't have any idea who it could have been?"

"Kid didn't say much of anything. Told us if we take him home he's just gonna run away again. Got a real chip on his shoulder."

I watched the cruiser pull out of the lot. Then I hopped in my car. The ride back took close to two hours. I kept thinking about the amusement park and the gunshots. I wondered what Petey wasn't telling and whether he had seen Susan's killer.

When we arrived at the Olivers all the lights seemed to be on in the house and a cruiser was parked in front. The outside light illuminated the front yard.

The front door opened and Petey's mother walked out onto the porch and down the steps.

I had met her once at the beginning of the school year. She was in her mid-forties, but with graying hair she appeared older. The baggy chinos and loose fitting black sweater she wore made it look like she had recently lost weight. Her face was caked with make-up, her expression determined. She walked quickly toward the cruiser.

Two cops hopped out. One of them opened the back door and motioned for Petey to get out. When he didn't the cop bent over and said something to him. Petey still didn't get out.

I got out of my car and began to walk toward the cruiser. The cop motioned me back and I leaned against my hood.

Mrs. Oliver took a few more steps toward the car. "Why won't he get out. What have you done to my son?"

I looked toward the porch. Nash and Cynthia Oliver stood silently, then Cynthia started down the stairs. "Get out of the car or I'm going to drag you out," she said.

Nash moved quickly down the steps and put his body between Cynthia and the cruiser. He whispered something in her ear. She stopped and glared at the car.

The cop talked to Petey for a few more seconds, then moved aside. Petey slid out of the back seat and stood looking at his mother.

She rushed over and put her arms around him. "We were so worried," she said.

Petey kept his arms at his side, lowered his head and walked slowly toward the house. His mother draped her hand over his shoulder, then let it drop. When he approached Cynthia his eyes narrowed. She took a step in his direction. The slap was so hard Petey's head snapped. He put his hand to his cheek and glared at her.

Nash moved quickly toward her, but before he could stop her she slapped Petey again. I moved toward her. Nash grabbed her shoulders and pushed her back.

"You get your hands off me," she said. "That son of a bitch killed my sister."

Nash pointed his finger inches from her face. "You touch him again and I'm taking you in. You hear me?"

Cynthia glared at him, then turned and walked a few feet up the sidewalk. Another cop took Petey by the arm and led him up the steps and into the house. Mrs. Oliver followed him in.

"Lieutenant," I said.

"I don't have time, Asher."

"Petey knows something he's not telling."

Nash took a deep breath. "I know," he said then headed toward the house. I followed. He turned and put his hand up. "Where do you think you're going?"

"I told Petey I'd stay with him."

"The Hadley police said the kid wasn't too appreciative of what you did. You're probably the last person he wants with him. Even if he did I couldn't allow it."

"Maybe he should have a lawyer."

Nash smiled. It looked out of place. "He's not being charged with anything. I just want to find out what he knows."

"You told me he's a suspect. Are you going to tell him his rights."

"Jesus, Asher. You want to help the kid then let me do my job." He climbed up onto the porch then turned and pointed his finger at me. "Go home."

"Petey's going to need protection," I said. "The guy that tried to get him at the amusement park isn't going to give up."

Nash walked into the house and slammed the door behind him.

I climbed back into my car and stared at the house. Two cops stood in the living room. Petey sat on the couch while his mother stood over him. Nash walked to the window and pulled down the shade.

I started my car, let it idle for a few seconds and watched as the Hadley Police drove away.

"Mr. Teacher." Cynthia Oliver walked in front of my car and put both hands on my hood. I put down the window.

"You stay out of my family's business."

"You get your kicks slapping little kids?"

"What I do to my brother is no concern of yours."

"How much did Aaron Fleming pay you to let him look at Susan's diary?"

Her face reddened. "I don't sell out my family. You think I like seeing Susan's name splashed all over the papers? No price is worth that."

"What she said about me wasn't true, but I don't imagine that matters to you."

"You knocked up my sister. I know that for a fact. I'm not through with you yet. None of my family is." She clenched her fist and banged it on the hood of my car. Then she turned and walked toward the house.

The anger I'd seen in Cynthia's face bothered me. I wondered what she meant by not being through with me yet. She'd given Susan's diary to Aaron. She couldn't do anything much worse. Or could she?

By the time I got home it was three a.m.. I could imagine the rumors that had flown around the school about why I wasn't in.

Richard cooed a welcome as I walked in the door. The message light on my answering machine indicated I had six messages. I punched the button.

The first three were from reporters wanting to talk to me. The fourth one was from James Carberry.

"It's important that I talk to you tonight," he said leaving a number. I wondered what McKinley's press secretary wanted this time.

The next message was from the Superintendent. "The school committee's agreed to hold off any meeting about you for now. I went out on a limb so, for Chrissake, don't get into anymore trouble."

I smiled then frowned as I recognized Aaron Fleming's voice. "All hell's broken loose. The McKinley people are blaming you. We've got to talk. Call me whenever you get in."

I looked at my watch. Aaron was the last person I felt like talking too. Whatever he wanted would have to wait.

I sat on the couch and rubbed my eyes. There hadn't been a message from Beth. I wanted to call her just to hear her voice, but it was too late. I'd wait until morning. I slipped the cassette out of the bag and popped it into my player. The screen turned bright blue for several seconds then an image slowly came into view. It was Susan Oliver.

CHAPTER 14

She was seated in an overstuffed gray chair. A rug was tacked to the wall behind her, covering most of the barnboard and a rocker sat next to a large wooden desk. I recognized the place as the Oliver cottage in Hadley.

Susan rubbed her right hand with her left. She was dressed in a light blue sweater and a plaid dress. The camera lens moved in to focus on her face. It was pale and her eyes bloodshot. She looked to the right for a second then focused on the camera.

"Edward McKinley and I have been lovers for the past four months." She let out a long sigh and her eyes welled up. "He said he loved me and promised to give me a job and financially take care of my family. I believed him. When he found out I was pregnant with his child he ordered me to have an abortion. I refused. He told me if I kept quiet until after the election he would divorce his wife and marry me. I didn't believe him for a second and told him. Later..." Tears rolled down her cheeks and she wiped them away. The camera closed in on her face. She choked back a sob and put her hand out to block the lens. "Chipper, I can't do this," she said. The screen turned bright blue.

I stared at it, then began to pace. Seeing Susan had shaken me. I sat on the couch and drummed my fingers along the arm. Who the hell was Chipper? He must be a friend of Susan's. Nash should be able to find out. I focused on what she said. Susan had lied about her relationship with me and I wasn't sure if I believed this story, but if McKinley had gotten her pregnant it was a pretty good motive for murder. Maybe Chipper would know what was going on.

I reached for the phone to call Fleming. I didn't care what time it was. Susan's image came back on the screen. Her hair had been brushed and she had put on lipstick.

"Edward McKinley is the father of my child. He has said he will deny it, but I have proof which I intend to turn over to the media as well as this tape. Everyone should know what a despicable human being he is." The screen turned blue again. I waited for more, then fast forwarded the tape. The rest was blank.

This tape had upset Petey enough to run away. I wondered why. If the story was true Susan had made a mistake. Petey was smart enough to see this, and from my talks with him, I knew he had witnessed worse things and was usually level headed. He must have recognized the cabin, but I couldn't figure why that would make him go out there.

I punched Fleming's number. "What's McKinley blaming me for?" I said when he got on the line.

He was silent for a few seconds then I heard the bed squeak. "Jesus, it's four-thirty in the morning."

"I know what time it is. I haven't been to bed yet. Start talking."

"The Globe's running a story in this morning's edition about an alleged affair between McKinley and Susan. Someone called them yesterday with a tip and rumors are flying. The paper spent the day checking it out. McKinley's denied it and a reporter I know over there called me looking for information about the diary, but mostly she wanted to know about you. She told me what McKinley's response is going to be. He's going to accuse you of slandering him to take suspicion off yourself in Susan's death. He's citing Susan's diary as proof."

"That's bullshit."

"They claim you set up a secret meeting with him on Sunday and tried to blackmail him. They have witnesses and they're saying it's not the only proof they have. They're gonna point out you were at the murder scene and my source says they know your motive for killing Susan. McKinley's holding a press conference tomorrow night. What the hell's going on, Steve?"

I banged my fist on the couch. "I don't know."

"Talk to me. Maybe I can help."

"The only reason you want to talk is so in tomorrow's paper you can say you had an exclusive interview with me?"

"You're in trouble," he said. "What I wrote was nothing. No one outside of Waltham cared if you and Susan dated, but implicating McKinley is another story. The press is going to be all over this. Look, McKinley has a lot of influential friends. He cultivates relationships so he can call in favors. Maybe he's convinced you're involved or maybe he just needs a scapegoat. Hell, it would be great publicity for his campaign if he helps find Susan's murderer. Point is, if he asks, the cops are going to come after you with a vengeance."

"So what should I do?"

"Hang low for now. Last thing you want to do is get involved in a media war with McKinley. He'd eat you alive. Wait and see what he says. Maybe I can help."

I thought about Lisa Gerrault and wondered if she had any idea what she was getting into when she agreed to represent me.

"When did the media know about Susan's pregnancy?"

"I don't understand."

"Just answer my question."

"I learned about it on Sunday. As far as I know it wasn't public knowledge until Monday. Why?"

"McKinley said he didn't know about it on Sunday afternoon. My gut tells me he was lying. Is there anyway he could have found out?"

"Jesus," he said. "What else did you guys talk about?"

"Just answer my question."

"It wasn't any secret. Sure he could have known, but what would that prove?"

I hesitated for a few seconds. "I'll get back to you."

I put my head back on the couch and closed my eyes. Things were moving too fast. I just wanted to crawl into bed for a week and sleep, but I couldn't. McKinley was going to use everything in his power to take suspicion off him. How could I prove he initiated the meeting on Sunday? They know your motive, Aaron had said. They couldn't have proof I was involved in anything unless Susan created it like the fantasy dates. The McKinley braintrust was already working to clear their man. I had to fight back.

I needed to call Beth and tell her what McKinley was going to do before she read it in the paper. I shook my head. Not now. I didn't have any way to prove it wasn't true.

I rewound the tape and pulled it out of the player. Nash's going to wonder why I didn't give it to the Hadley police. With the Globe story the timing of my turning it over looked bad. Petey had to tell them he found it, but as far as I knew Petey wasn't talking. I stared at the phone for a few seconds then called the police and left a message for Nash. Lisa Gerrault had told me not to talk to the cops without her being present. I looked at my watch and shook my head. All I intended to do was turn the cassette over to Nash. If he wanted to ask me questions about Susan's diary I'd call Lisa. Ten minutes later the phone rang.

"What've you got?" He sounded tired.

"A video of Susan. It's what upset Petey enough to run away."

"Give me an hour."

I took a shower and let the water run over my body. The exhaustion I felt earlier had left me and I felt wired, like the last thing I needed was sleep. By the time I got back into the kitchen it was close to six. I refilled Richard's water and spread some birdseed on the floor of his cage. He seemed quieter than usual as if he knew something was wrong.

I wolfed down a handful of Cheerios. I wasn't hungry. I just needed to be doing something.

The sound of a car stopping in front of the house caught my attention and I heard the paper hitting the walkway. I felt a knot tighten in my stomach as I went outside and picked it up. I expected to see my name splashed on the front page. The top story was about Petey being found, but there was nothing about McKinley. I spread the paper out on the kitchen table and went through it. A small article on page 12 mentioned Susan's diary and my connection. They quoted my denial and that some of her friends said we had dated. It didn't mention McKinley. There was nothing in the rest of the paper. "What the hell was Fleming talking about," I said aloud.

I read the story about Petey. It didn't mention my name or the gunman at the amusement park. I turned on the all news radio station. Petey was the top story. Again my name didn't come up. I punched Fleming's number. "What happened to your big story?" I said.

"I'm as surprised as you are. The Globe must have sat on it. The Herald didn't have anything either. Maybe they got some facts to check out."

"Or maybe they found out it's not true," I said.

"Believe me, they're gonna run it. The McKinley people are all geared up for it. I'll check with my reporter friend. See what happened. When I find out I'll let you know."

Five minutes later Nash arrived. His hair was disheveled and his tie hung loose on his shirt. Richard cooed a welcome, but he ignored him. "Show me."

I handed him the tape and explained what was on it. He studied the cassette for a few seconds then slipped it into the player. As it played he remained silent. From his expression I couldn't tell what he was thinking. When it was over he rewound it and began to watch it again. As the first image of Susan came on he pressed pause and moved closer to the screen. He examined the table next to Susan. Something was on it, but the picture was so fuzzy I couldn't make out what it was.

"It was taken at the Oliver cabin in Hadley," I said.

He punched the play button. Every few seconds he pressed pause and studied the film. When it ended he rewound it and took it out of the machine.

"Any idea who Chipper might be?" he said.

"Must be a friend of Susan's. Shouldn't be too hard to find him."

"Someone stole cassettes from your house." It wasn't a question just a statement. "Why would this upset the kid enough to run away?"

"From what I know about Petey it shouldn't have. Unless he recognized the cabin and had a reason to go out there. What did he say to you?"

Nash's eyes narrowed as if he were thinking and he looked toward the wall. "I won't talk about what Petey said, but I'll tell you this. I find it kind of strange that you just happen to know where the kid was hiding."

I shrugged. "I explained it to the Hadley cops."

"I know, but I still don't buy it. It'd make more sense if Petey called you, told you where he was and asked you to go get him."

"That's not the way it happened. If I was going to meet him it wouldn't be in a deserted amusement park where I could be followed by someone with a gun. The Hadley police have any luck finding the guy?"

"You'll have to ask them. Right now I've got my hands full."

I resisted the urge to point out the man could have been Susan's killer. Nash knew that and he also knew what the Hadley Police were doing. "Did Susan's diary mention McKinley?"

"You're the second person to ask me that. We'll look into this, believe me. I read Fleming's article on you and I've talked to him." He paused. "Actually he went kind of light on you. The diary gave a lot of specifics about your relationship."

"Such as?"

He shook his head.

"None of it's true," I said.

"How'd she know about your birthmark?"

"I don't know."

He studied me as if waiting for more. "Believe me, if I was certain about things I'd take you in now." He turned and headed for the door.

"I've got a lawyer and I'm getting tired of this."

He turned back to me. "So am I. I've been doing some checking on you. Arrested when you were twenty-one for drunk and disorderly. Released into the custody of your mother. Not much of a rap sheet. You're not used to being in trouble with the law."

I smiled and a sense of release flooded over me.

"What's so amusing?" Nash said.

"I'm not a murderer," I said. "I wouldn't even consider it for a hobby."

His eyes narrowed. "Is everything a joke with you?"

"No," I said. "I'm sorry. Susan's death isn't a joke. Sometimes that's the way I deal with the pain."

He nodded.

"Lieutenant. You might as well hear this from me. According to a reporter I know the McKinley people are going to say I leaked a story about him and Susan to the press. I..."

He held up his hand. "I've already talked to his press secretary on the phone. He was looking for information. Seemed to think he was an important man. Didn't get far with that approach."

"I just want you to know whatever you hear is not true."

"Hard to believe that everybody's lying" He walked out the door.

I poured another cup of coffee and sat at the kitchen table. That Nash didn't find any police record from my college days made me feel better, but he was right. It would be hard for the cops to believe everyone was lying. I ran things through my mind from the beginning right up to Susan's video and McKinley saying he knew my motive for killing Susan. Someone was trying to frame me for her murder. Maybe that's why they didn't kill me at the cabin. They needed me alive. I wondered what they had planned next and how far were they willing to go. But the more important question was how could I stop them.

CHAPTER 15

I sat for awhile longer trying to work things out in my mind. I felt reluctant to go to school, but I knew I had to. I was lost in thought when the doorbell rang.

I looked out the window. It was Beth. It was unusual for her to come over this early.

"Is everything all right?" I said as I opened the door.

"I heard it on the radio," she said. "Are you okay?"

"I'm fine. The radio didn't mention my name. How did you know?"

"I called the school yesterday and they told me you'd taken personal leave. I swung by a few times and your car wasn't in the yard. When I heard Petey had been found I knew where you went."

"Come on up," I said. "I'll make some fresh coffee?"

She walked up the stairs and sat on the couch. Her body was rigid and she rested her hands on her lap. I sat beside her. She was dressed in jeans and a gray sweatshirt that had a Picasso print on the front. I explained about finding Petey and the video he gave me. I didn't mention the guy with the gun. I didn't want her to tell me how stupid I had been to go to the park alone. When I was through she said. "Do you believe what Susan said on the video?"

I shrugged. "She lied about me. She could be lying about McKinley too." I studied her for a few seconds. "What's really on your mind."

She rubbed her arm with her hand. "What I have to say isn't easy, but I had to tell you face to face." She looked away for a few seconds then refocused on me. "I wanted it to work for us. I really did. But it just doesn't feel right. Sometimes I want to be with you so much and the next minute I want you out of my life."

I looked at her for a few seconds. Her words didn't sink in. Then

I realized what she said. "What are you talking about? Sure we've had a few problems, but we'll work them out."

She held her hand up. "Let me finish."

"No, I've heard enough."

"There you go again." She raised her voice. "You never want to deal with problems. At the first sign of trouble you always pull away. You keep things inside and won't talk.

"None of what's being said is true. It'll be cleared up as soon as the cops find who killed Susan."

"You don't get it, Steve. That's not why I'm doing this. I've been thinking about it for a few weeks. I just didn't want to face it. The problem is you. You don't want to grow up and take any responsibility. When you have a problem you won't talk to me and sometimes I get the feeling you're living in your own private world. I can't stay in a relationship where I have to guess what you're thinking." She shook her head. "I need openness. Someone who cares about me and making himself better. You just want to listen to your music and let your life slide by."

I felt my anger start to rise. "You're the most important thing in my life, but I'm a little preoccupied now."

"Will you listen to me?" she said. "It's more than just us. You can't sit back anymore. You've got to act, show some initiative. Twenty years ago you were passive. I'll deal with the charges if they surface you told me. A lot of people believe Susan's story. You've got to deal with it."

"For Chrissake. I've got a lawyer. I found Petey. What else do you want me to do?"

"You can stop feeling sorry for yourself."

"Damn it. Tell me what you think I should do and I'll do it."

She shook her head. "This sounds so familiar."

"Right. We had this same argument six years ago." I tried to keep my voice from shaking. "Stay. We can work things out."

She pushed her hair back from her forehead and shook her head. "I know you're in trouble. If you need someone to talk to you can call."

I got up and paced. "Look, I'm sorry. It's such a shock. I really thought things were going to work. You're the one always talking about openness. If breaking up has been on your mind for weeks how come you never told me?"

"I guess I was hoping it would work, too." She got up. "You sure you're okay?"

I nodded.

"I was scared coming over here. I was afraid I'd change my mind at the last minute and we'd go on for another six months. It's better this way." She kissed me lightly on the cheek, then looked at Richard's cage for a few seconds and walked out the door.

I listened as her footsteps faded and her car started. Then I put my head back and closed my eyes. There was a time, right after my divorce, when I specialized in one-night stands as if I had to prove something to myself. Then I came to the realization that I only wanted one woman in my life and that was Beth. I thought about the past few months. How come I didn't see this coming? She said it wasn't connected to Susan's death, but it sure seemed like it. Maybe she's right. Maybe I was too passive, just waiting for things to happen. I wouldn't let things end for us. If the cops couldn't clear me, I'd do it myself. I'd prove to Beth how wrong she is. Then I'd fight to get her back.

I was fifteen minutes late for school. I went into the office, grabbed my mail and tried to make a quick exit.

Mary, the principal's secretary, looked up from her computer. "Mr. Webster would like to see you." She refocused on the screen.

When I entered Webster's office he was seated behind his desk, talking on the phone. He held up one finger and motioned for me to sit down.

The office had a wall of bookcases on the right. Pictures of his wife and two kids plus several framed certificates lined it. One honored him as Man of the Year from the Kiwanis Club and another for his volunteer work with The Red Cross. He smiled at me as he talked. I'd seen that smile before. It meant he was unhappy with something I'd done.

He hung up the phone and stared at me for a few seconds. Webster was tall and gaunt. His gray hair was cut short and his suit pulled tight around him as he pushed back in his chair. "I've got someone covering your first class," he said. "We thought you weren't coming in."

"Sorry I'm late. I got tied up." I almost smiled as an image of what I said flashed through my mind. "I'm going to need coverage so I can go to Susan's funeral."

Webster rested his hands on the desk. "I want you to know I think the Superintendent's making a mistake by not suspending you and I let him and the School Committee know my feelings. I convinced some of the committee members that it's in the kid's best interests if you're not in the classroom for a few days."

"Thanks for your show of support."

"I'm going to ask them to meet tonight."

"Are you through?"

"No. I'm not through. There were reporters here yesterday looking for you. They wanted to talk to anyone who knew you. They were bothering the kids. We can't have these kind of disruptions."

"You usually like having the press here."

His face turned red and he paused for several seconds. Then he said, "Things would be easier on your students if you took some time off. They can't concentrate when every day they read something about their teacher in the paper."

"I'm going back to my classroom. I'll let you know when I'm leaving."

He pushed back in his chair. "I'm just trying to do what's best for everyone involved."

"So am I. Everything you've heard is a lie and I'm not going to run away from this. I'm going to fight to prove my innocence. That's the lesson I want kids to learn."

He nodded. "I understand, but you'll save yourself some bad headlines if you quietly take some personal time. Maybe things will calm down and the committee won't have to suspend you."

"That's out of the question."

"Then I'm pressing the committee to suspend you and believe me, I have the votes. It's your reputation."

"That's right. It is my reputation and I'm not going to let you or the committee destroy it."

I walked slowly toward my classroom. Webster had gotten me angry before and we've had a few arguments, especially when I was the Teacher's Union Representative, but today he really pissed me off. His major concern has always been his school's image. His desire for favorable newspaper stories was well known. Disruptions made his school look bad. He once told me "A quiet classroom is a good classroom." He didn't care about a teacher's personal problems. He just wanted them to show up on time.

A locker door was ajar and I slammed it so hard it bounced back open. I stared at it for a few seconds. What the hell was I doing? I seemed to be losing control of everything around me. When I go into my classroom I don't want to take my anger out on the kids. They were the reason I was still here.

I went into the men's room and splashed water on my face. I looked in the mirror and noted the dark circles under my eyes. I straightened my tie and went back out in the hallway. Two long fluorescent lights ran along the high ceiling, casting shadows on the beige tile walls. No one was in the corridor. I enjoyed the silence, if only for a few minutes.

When I entered my room the kids were silently reading. Bob Driscoll, the shop teacher, sat at my desk.

"Where've you been, Mr. A.," a student said.

"I had some business to take care of, Frank."

Driscoll got up, squeezed my shoulder and walked out of the room. Twenty-two faces stared at me.

I smiled. "The good news is Petey has been found and is back with his family." Some students nodded, others grinned while several showed little emotion.

"Were you dating Petey's sister, Mr. A.?"

The silence seemed to last a long time before I shook my head. "No, I wasn't and I don't know why Susan wrote that in her diary."

"My mother said the school board's going to suspend you."

I walked to the blackboard, picked up a piece of chalk and tossed it in the air. "They could, but I'm going to make them see that they'd be making a mistake." I turned and wrote 1692 on the blackboard. "Anyone know what happened in that year?"

"The witches," Billy said.

"That's right." I walked up the row toward Billy's desk. "What can you tell me about it?"

Billy put his hands on the side of the desk. "People were accused of doing things they didn't do. A lot of the stories were made up and people were hanged."

""That's right. Why would people make up stories?" I flipped the piece of chalk toward Karl.

He caught it. "Maybe they wanted attention or maybe they did it because all their friends were telling stories and they didn't want to be left out."

"Good," I said catching the piece of chalk Karl threw back. "Can you think of any other reasons?"

Brenda raised her hand. I flipped her the chalk. "Maybe there were some people they didn't like so they made up stories about them."

"Beautiful," I said. "Brenda, write all of these reasons on the board."

We watched her for a couple of minutes. "Any witch jokes, Mr. A.?"

"Sure. Do you know how witches tell time? They look at their witch watch."

I love eighth grade humor.

When Brenda finished I said, "Could any of the stories be true?"

Natalie raised her hand. "Maybe. We just don't have enough information."

"How 'bout if we cut the crap," Brandon said from the back row.

All eyes turned toward him. He was slouched back in his chair with his arms folded across his chest and his feet sticking out in the aisle.

"What's on your mind, Brandon?" I said.

"How 'bout if you stop playing games with us. We're talking about you, not witches and I think you're lying about Petey's sister."

I nodded. "Anyone else think I'm lying?"

No hands went up, but I could tell by several expressions that they either agreed or weren't sure.

"No one's gonna admit it," Brandon said. "You'd probably flunk 'em."

I wiped some chalk dust on my pants. "No, I wouldn't. Everyone has a right to their own opinion. All I'm asking is that you keep an open mind, get all the facts and then reach your own decision."

"I have," Brandon said. "I think you did it and I think you're conning us. Mr. Doucette thinks so too. I heard him talking to Mrs. O' Connor in the hallway."

I tried to keep the anger out of my voice. "The cops will get Susan's killer and it's not me."

Brandon gave a low laugh and turned away.

I put the chalk back in the tray. I was losing some of these kids. If the investigation goes on much longer how many others will look at me suspiciously and stop listening.

I asked the students to write a story telling me about a time they might have been falsely accused of something and how it made them feel. Brandon turned his back and didn't write. The rest worked quietly. Several stared at me for a few seconds as if thinking. I noticed notes being passed around, but I didn't take them.

The incident with Brandon had shaken me. I've had run-ins with students before. All teachers have, but this one was more personal and I almost lost my temper. Maybe Webster was right. How can I teach if some of my students don't trust me?

When the bell rang several students left. The rest didn't move. Out in the hallway other students laughed, talked loudly and slammed lockers.

Natalie got to her feet. Everyone stared at her. "We're behind you, Mr. A.," she said. "Give 'em hell." She walked to my desk and put a piece of lined paper on it.

It said, "If the school board suspends you we're going to go to a meeting and tell them what a good teacher you are." It was signed by about two-thirds of the class.

I felt a lump form in my throat. "Thank you," was all I could say.

There were only a few cars in the parking lot of the funeral home when I arrived. I sat in my car for a few minutes. My mind flashed to Susan's father. He had stopped paying child support years ago and the family hadn't been able to track him down. I wondered if he knew about Susan's death and if he'd come to the funeral.

Inside, the first thing that caught my eye was the closed casket. Susan's mother and Petey sat in folding chairs to the left. A few people stood around talking quietly. Two men in dark suits stood close to the family. One I recognized as a cop on the Waltham force. He nodded toward me. I wondered where Cynthia was.

Petey's head was tilted toward his mother and they were talking. Neither looked up as I walked to the casket and kneeled. I felt a tightening in my stomach as I said a silent prayer for Susan. Then

I walked over to Mrs. Oliver and shook her hand.

She smiled, but her eyes were glazed. "Thank you for coming."

"I'm sorry about Susan," I said.

She closed her eyes and looked away. I wasn't even sure if she knew who I was.

Petey was dressed in a dark blue suit, white shirt and a red tie. His hair, which usually fell over his forehead, was slicked back.

"You look pretty sharp," I said.

He got up and shook my hand. "I'm sorry about how I acted. You were right." He nodded toward Susan's casket. "I should be here for this."

Mrs. Oliver turned to talk to another woman. I leaned close to Petey's ear. "We have to talk about the video, but not now."

He nodded.

A young woman entered the room. She was dressed in a dark blue skirt and white blouse. Her eyes were red. She looked toward the casket, then to Mrs. Oliver. Her mouth opened but nothing came out.

Mrs. Oliver put her hand on the woman's shoulder. Then they hugged.

The woman walked slowly to the coffin, kneeled and bowed her head for several seconds. When she got up she staggered slightly. I took her by the arm and steadied her.

"This is so hard," she said. "I'm Molly Franklin." She extended her hand. "I don't think we've met."

"I'm Steve Asher."

Her eyes narrowed and she pulled away. "Why are you lying about Susan?"

"I'm not lying."

"Oh yes you are." Her voice rose and several people turned in our direction. "She told me you didn't want anyone to know, but she's dead now. How can you be so inhuman?"

Before I could respond a loud voice sounded from around the corner of the hallway. It was Cynthia Oliver. "You've no business being here," she screamed. For a split second I thought she was yelling at me.

One of the cops moved quickly around the corner and toward the noise.

"You should talk," a male voice said. "You're the hypocrite."

I heard a loud crash and a man grunted. Mrs. Oliver got to her feet and covered her mouth with her hand. Molly moved beside her and gently touched her arm.

I went out to the hallway to see what was happening. A cop had his arms around Cynthia Olivers' shoulders. She flailed her arms trying to break loose. A man in his thirties stood inches in front of her. He had thinning brown hair, a paunch and a long sharp nose. The gray suit he wore pulled tightly around his pear-shaped body.

He moved closer and pointed a finger at her. "You haven't been home in five years. How would you know what Susan wanted? It sickens me that you're playing the grieving sister. At least I cared for her while we were married and I still care for her."

Cynthia's eyes narrowed. "If you cared so much why'd she have to get the restraining order?"

"She didn't need one to keep you away," he said. "You wouldn't have anything to do with her. Don't forget I know the real story."

He straightened his tie and ran his fingers over his hair trying to cover a bald spot. Then he turned and walked toward the main room. I followed him.

When he rounded the corner Mrs. Oliver jumped to her feet. "Don't let him near my daughter," she yelled.

CHAPTER 16

The two cops walked quickly into the parlor, stopped and stared at the man.

He stood in front of the coffin with his head down. His body sagged slightly. Then he turned and approached Mrs. Oliver. He put his arm on her shoulder and leaned close to her face. "Madeline, I'm so sorry."

She pulled away and her eyes narrowed. "You don't belong here," she said.

"I know, I know. I tried to keep away. I didn't want to upset anyone, but I couldn't." He pointed to the casket. "Let me just say good-bye." He moved toward the coffin, kneeled in front of it and bowed his head for a few seconds.

The two cops moved behind Mrs. Oliver. Cynthia entered the room and stood in the doorway, her eyes fastened on the man. The door to the funeral parlor slammed. It was the only sound in the room.

The man rose, turned and approached Mrs. Oliver again. She looked away. Molly glared at him. "You know how much I cared for her," he said.

Molly walked out of the room.

He closed his eyes for a second. "I'm sorry for upsetting you," he said quietly. "I just want to help any way I can."

Mrs. Oliver refocused on him. Her eyes narrowed and her face turned red. "Don't think you're riding in the limo."

"No. No. I wouldn't think of it."

"I don't even want you at the cemetery." She waved her hand as if dismissing him.

The man nodded and looked at Petey. "Aren't you going to at least say hello to me?"

Petey turned away.

The man shrugged and looked at me. "Damon Saulnier," he said extending his hand.

"I'm Steve Asher."

I took his hand and shook it. A heavy gold signet ring gleamed on his finger. I noticed a momentary flicker in his eyes. "You found Susan."

I nodded.

"I've heard things about you, but it doesn't matter much now, does it?" he said. "It's such a terrible tragedy for all of us."

I wanted to say it did matter. Ask him if Susan made up lies about other men. Ask him about the restraining order and how he felt knowing that she had been pregnant, but this wasn't the time. Instead I just nodded.

Cynthia moved into the room toward him. "I'm not going to put up with this. My sister divorced you five years ago and the only time she heard from you is when you needed money. Now you show up pretending you care. How 'bout helping us pay for burying her if you loved her so much?"

He smiled. "Cynthia, why do you always act like an immature teenager? I'm going to leave, but only out of respect for your mother. Susan's dead, for Chrissake. Can't you put aside your anger for just one day?"

They stared at each other for a few seconds, then he turned, put his arm on my shoulder and motioned with his head for me to move out into the hallway. When I did he said, "I'm sorry for your loss too." Then he moved his face close to my ear. "If I find out you had anything to do with this I won't wait for the police to arrest you. I'll kill you myself. Understand, Pal?" He turned and walked out the door.

I followed him. "I don't like being threatened," I said.

He turned and the smile was back on his face. "Not a threat. Just a statement of fact."

"Susan lied about me," I said. "Did she lie about other men too?"

He shook his head. "You can say nothing happened to the cops, but don't bullshit me. Susan was a lot of things, but a liar wasn't one of them. Hell, if she even tried, her face turned red and she'd start to stutter. If she said you dated, I believe her."

"Why'd she get a restraining order?"

"None of your business, Asher. I'll tell you this, though. That family is crazy. The police should be investigating them. You get on the wrong side of that group and they'll come at you so fast you won't know it happened." He hesitated. "When I first heard Susan was dead I didn't believe it. The family has a history of making up stories. You might want to ask Cynthia about that." He began to laugh. "Yeah, ask Cynthia."

Two men walked out of the funeral home and stared at us. Damon got in his car and drove away.

I went to my car and waited for the procession to start. Saulnier's threat bothered me and I wondered what he meant about the family having a history of making up stories. What else had they lied about?

The casket was loaded into the hearse. When the Olivers came out I focused on Cynthia. Her gaze darted around the parking lot. She seemed more nervous than mournful. Then they got into the limo.

It started to drizzle as the cars pulled out of the lot. After a funeral service at Sacred Heart Church the hearse detoured to drive by the Oliver house. Five cars and the limo followed.

About a dozen people gathered at Cavalry Street Cemetery. I stood behind them and watched as the coffin was unloaded and placed into the grave. A priest recited a prayer, then said a few words about Susan. One by one, Madeline, Cynthia and then Petey laid roses on the casket. Tears rolled down Mrs. Oliver's cheeks. Neither of her children tried to comfort her. I wanted to go and wrap my arms around her. I thought about how unfair it was that Susan was the second child Madeline Oliver had lost.

A thick row of maples lined the edge of the cemetery a few hundred feet from where Susan was being buried. Out of the corner of my eye I saw a man dressed in a dark suit walk out of trees. He had a mustache and his hair covered his ears. He moved slowly toward us and then stopped. He appeared to be in his early twenties, and although I could barely see his face, there was something about him that was familiar. I watched him for a few seconds then refocused on the family.

Cynthia looked over at the trees. Her eyes widened and she shook her head. I looked back toward the man. He waved at her, took a step toward the crowd, then stopped.

The ceremony ended and people slowly headed back to their cars. The priest talked quietly to Madeline while Petey stood next to her with his hands shoved into his pockets. Cynthia looked toward the man by the trees then moved quickly to the limo. The man turned and walked into the woods.

I got into my car. The mourners had been invited back to the Olivers, but I had to get back to school.

I took one last look at the open grave. Instead of driving toward the main entrance I took a road which led to the rear. Based on the direction the guy had disappeared, he had to park near here. I was planning to get his plate number and turn it over to the police, but he had already left. Asher, I said to myself, you're getting paranoid. The guy could have had a legitimate reason not to join the mourners, but I had to admit I was intrigued.

It was lunchtime and I picked up a Quarter Pounder with cheese and a Coke, then headed back to school. Beth was on my mind. I thought about going to her house and telling her how much I needed her, asking her to give me another chance. But I couldn't. Not until the cops found Susan's killer.

I parked around the back of the school and went in the rear door. My confrontation with Brandon still bothered me and the expressions I had seen on several students' faces made me wonder if I could be an effective teacher while the police searched for Susan's killer. Maybe Webster was right. Maybe I was too controversial to be a productive teacher right now. I did know that if I felt my staying in the classroom was hurting the kids I would have no choice. I'd take personal leave even if it looked like I had something to hide.

When I walked into the teachers' room the conversation quieted. No one asked me to join them for lunch and no one asked about Susan's diary. A few turned away and those that spoke seemed distant. If I'd had any doubts before, that showed me how serious the damage was from the stories that had been in the paper.

I went back to my room and sat alone munching on my burger. I was starting to feel rebellious and angry. When the door opened I didn't look up.

"How come you're eating by yourself?" It was Frank Oullette, the English teacher.

"Why?"

"People are asking about you," he said. "You all right?"

"No, I'm not all right. I'm beginning to feel guilty. What's the word out there? Did I kill Susan?"

He shut the door and sat on one of the desks. Frank and I had started at North on the same day. He was one of my close friends at school. On paydays we'd always go out and have a few drinks. Not only did I like him, but I respected his judgment. "People are confused, Steve. You're not being open with them and they don't know what to think."

"That's the way I am Frank. I'm not going to jump up and down and say I didn't do it. Shit, I've worked with some of you for twelve years. By now you should know what kind of guy I am."

"If it's any consolation I don't think you had anything to do with it, but, yeah, some people do. They think it might be better if you take a leave of absence till things are straightened out."

"Did Webster put you up to this?"

He shook his head. "I'm here on my own. I'm just telling you what I'm hearing."

"Thanks, Frank. I don't mean to take things out on you. It's just starting to get to me."

He got off the desk and put his hand on my shoulder. "You want to stop for a beer after school?"

I shook my head.

"I'm buying."

"I've got some things I want to do."

He nodded, then headed for the door. "Don't shut us all out. I'll be around after school if you change your mind."

I taught my last two classes. Some students seemed preoccupied and I tried to include them in discussions to gage their reaction toward me. By the end of the school day I still wasn't sure what to do.

I flipped on an all news station as I headed home. At the top of the hour the headlines came on. The first story was about McKinley. "Edward McKinley will hold a major press conference tonight," the reporter said. "He's expected to make an important announcement. Rumors have been circulating all day that he is going to pull out of the Governor's race. McKinley canceled all appearances today. Members of his staff have been unavailable for comment. We'll have more details as soon as they're available."

CHAPTER 17

I stepped hard on the accelerator. If McKinley was really dropping out of the race it would have to be because of Susan. Carberry had wanted to talk last night. He'd left his number on my machine.

Richard was noisier than usual as I entered the apartment. I tapped on his cage. He cocked his head and cooed.

I retrieved Carberry's number and left a message when I got his machine. The card with McKinley's car phone number still lay on the coffee table. I punched it out, but no one answered. Then I called Aaron Fleming at the Trib.

"Any idea what's going on?" I said.

"You talking to me now?"

"It's my day to talk to assholes."

He laughed. "No one knows. The press conference is tonight at the Park Plaza. Rumors have been circulating all day about a relationship McKinley had with Susan Oliver. According to my source McKinley's denying it and is gonna take the offensive. My guess is your name is going to come up. I know I'm not going to miss it."

"The radio said he might be pulling out of the race."

"Not according to what I heard."

"Take me along."

"No can do. First, they won't let you in without press credentials, and second, security is going to be real tight. I couldn't sneak you in even if I wanted to."

"Get me some credentials."

"Impossible. Not for this event. I'd lose my job."

"How 'bout if I make it worth your while? If McKinley is going after me I want to be there to answer what he says. I'll give you the exclusive interview you want. You told me you're bored working for the Tribune anyway. They might do you a favor by firing you."

He let out a long sigh. "I wish there was a way."

"Did your source say why the Globe didn't print the story this morning?"

"She didn't, but my guess is they want to be sure what they have is accurate. Plus McKinley may feel he owes them a favor for sitting on the story until he has a chance to organize his rebuttal. I'm sure the paper could figure out a way to take advantage of it.

"I'm still waiting for your notes from Susan's diary."

"You know I won't do that."

"You're sure Susan wrote it?"

"Yeah. We had the handwriting checked. It's hers all right."

"When was the last entry?"

"A couple of days before she was killed."

"Hang on," I said flipping back the calendar and pinpointing the date I met Susan for coffee. "What does she have down for November 2?"

I heard the rustling of paper then he said, "Work was more boring than usual today. Met Steve for coffee. At least he brings excitement into my life. Back to his apartment afterwards."

"Jesus." I paused. "Does she ever mention McKinley?"

"Never. Believe me I checked. Look I gotta run."

I put on a Del Shannon C.D. and tried to relax, but I couldn't. I kept thinking about McKinley's press conference and Susan's diary. Someone knew why she was lying about me. I had to find out who that someone was.

The ringing of the phone jarred me. It was James Carberry. "We know you leaked the story to the press."

"You're wrong about that. If anyone leaked the story it was a member of the Oliver family or maybe even one of your own staff. Is McKinley dropping out of the race?"

"Absolutely not. Ed had nothing to do with Susan and you know it. He's gonna prove it tonight."

"If he comes out after me he's going to make a big mistake."

"That's what I told him. I said ignore it. Don't justify it with a denial. But he's innocent and he wants to take it head on. He believes you're the one responsible."

"I'm not the person to go after, but I think he's doing the right thing. He's got to respond to the rumors. It would look worse if he didn't, but he has to handle it right."

He lowered his voice. "Ed doesn't know I called and if you mention it I'll deny it. I need your help."

"Why?"

"I'll do whatever it takes to help my candidate win. What we need is for the truth to come out. You knew Susan and you know Ed wasn't involved with her. You gotta tell people how unstable she was. They'll believe you because you're not connected with the campaign."

"I don't know that she was unstable."

"Don't bullshit me. This is the campaign issue Frank Mitchell's been waiting for." He lowered his voice. "Ed's got people investigating you. If he finds anything he'll eat you alive. I'm trying to head that off. It'll be better for everyone."

"And you don't care about Susan's reputation."

He hesitated. "She's the one that got herself involved with her lies."

"Tell me what you have in mind."

"I want you to meet privately with Ed before his press conference. Just the three of us to talk things out. It'll cool everyone off and maybe we can convince you to talk to the press about Susan."

"What's in it for me?"

"Maybe you can convince Ed you're not the one who did this to him."

"Can I bring someone?"

"Sure, but the meeting is going to be just the three of us. No outsiders."

"You may be surprised at how little I know about Susan."

"That's not what it says in her diary?"

"I know what's in it. We'll talk tonight."

"Fine. Be at the campaign headquarters on Tremont Street about six-thirty." He hung up.

I sat on the couch and rubbed my eyes. I had felt relief when Nash hadn't found anything in the police files about me. But now McKinley was looking. Suppose he talks to someone who knew me in college and remembers the rumors. McKinley wouldn't hesitate to use it. If he told the media or mentioned it at his press conference tonight how could I prove that a twenty year old story was false. It's the last thing I wanted the school committee to hear.

I called Aaron Fleming. "I want a copy of your notes, and now I've got something to trade. I'm having a private meeting with McKinley and Carberry before tonight's press conference. You give me the notes and I'll bring you."

"Do I get to sit in on the meeting?"

"I would imagine McKinley's pretty anxious to get a look at what's in the diary. If the only way he can see it is by having you in the meeting, I think he'd do it. Besides I think Carberry's not being honest with me about why he wants to meet and I'd like someone else sitting in on it."

"Steve, you got yourself a deal."

I grabbed a Coke from the refrigerator and sat on the couch. McKinley didn't need political advice from me. He had lots of advisors he could turn to. I rubbed the can against my cheek. I felt nervous about the meeting, but I had to go and tell my side. Truth was, nothing I could say would stop McKinley from going after me if he believed I was leaking stories to the press. What the hell was Carberry up to?

I put on an Eddie Cochran C.D. and dressed to "Summertime Blues." Then I checked Richard's water supply. "I'd take you to the press conference," I said, "but you'd probably cause a scene."

Aaron's blue Toyota pulled up in front of my apartment at six and he honked the horn. I went downstairs and slid into the front seat. "You got your notes?"

He nodded.

"Can I see them?"

"I still don't feel right about this. Why do you think Carberry's gonna let me sit in on your meeting?"

I told him what Carberry had said on the phone.

"I told you the diary doesn't mention McKinley. I've made up my mind, Steve. You'll only see it if I get into the meeting."

I nodded then smiled. "The mustache's new," I said.

"Makes me look older, don't you think? Kinda like a young Burt Reynolds."

"Makes you look like an eighteen year old who needs a shave."

"Gonna be thirty next month. Never thought at this age I'd still be working for the Trib."

Aaron was no more than five-eight, with a round face, red hair
and freckles. He looked more like Opie on the Andy Griffth show
than Burt Reynolds, but his innocent good looks seemed to charm
lots of women. He wore a Red Sox warm-up jacket, chinos and
Nikes.

"Nice of you to dress up for the meeting."

"McKinley's a big Sox fan. I thought I'd try to impress him."

We followed Main Street through Watertown, then pulled onto
Storrow Drive. I watched the skyscrapers loom in the distance.
Aaron had his radio tuned to a jazz station.

"Carberry's idea is just crazy enough to make some kind of
sense," he said. "Why don't you believe him?"

"He didn't become McKinley's press secretary by doing things
without his knowledge. He got the job by being ruthless and keeping his boss happy. I think McKinley told him to set up this meeting. I just don't know why. What's your take on the rumors about
him and Susan?"

"No way he had an affair with her. People have been trying to dig
up dirt on him for years and never found anything. Guy's a boy
scout. Perfect wife, perfect kids. He's tough, though. If he finds out
who spread the rumors, he'll tear them apart."

"I got a feeling he thinks it's me."

We exited Storrow and stopped at a red light beside the Public
Gardens.

"Maybe Susan just got to him," I said.

Aaron shook his head. "McKinley's got his sights set on
Washington. Being Governor is just the first step. The timing's all
wrong. Besides the guy's never been known as a womanizer. He
doesn't smoke and doesn't drink anything stronger than Pepsi.
Been married to his high school sweetheart for thirty years. When
they're together they still hold hands, for Chrissake. His whole
campaign is based on family values. It just doesn't make sense for
him to get involved with Susan."

"So who do you think is spreading the rumors?"

He looked at me, but didn't respond.

We found a parking space on Commonwealth and walked the few
blocks to headquarters. It was just after six-thirty when we entered.
A dozen people were standing around talking. I recognized the

woman I talked to on Sunday. She leaned closer to the group and lowered her voice when she saw me.

I looked for Carberry or McKinley, but there was no sign of them. "I've got a meeting with Mr. McKinley," I said to Meg.

Her eyes narrowed. "He's been delayed," she said then went on whispering.

I sat in a folding chair by the wall. Aaron pulled out his note pad and walked over to the group.

The office looked the same as the last time I was in it except there seemed to be more campaign posters. Several folding chairs had been set up against the wall. A door to a back room had the word "office" stenciled on it.

A cardboard box sat on a table in the middle of the room. It was bulky, perhaps three feet long and almost as high. Strips of brown tape were wrapped erratically around it and a Federal Express sticker was on the side. Sharp Video Player was printed on the side.

When I refocused on Aaron he was talking quietly to an attractive blonde woman. He spent a few more minutes with her then came and sat beside me.

"She's kinda cute, don't you think?"

I shook my head. "You probably go to family reunions to pick up women."

He smiled. "By the time we were through talking we'd sort of established a relationship. The next time I need information we're gonna be old friends."

"You ask her out?"

"Hell, no. I was just getting a little background on what his workers are thinking. They're worried, but the line is they've got great faith in Ed. Meg's filling them in on your connection with Susan."

"I'm sure she is."

"Look, I need a cigarette," Aaron said. "I'll be outside. If I see McKinley I'll come back."

I got up, went to a coffee machine and poured myself a cup. The blonde came over to join me. The others turned to watch her.

"You're working for him, aren't you?" she said.

"Who?"

"Frank Mitchell. You'll do anything to get him the nomination."

"What I'm doing is not political at all. If McKinley wins it'll be because more people think he's the right person for the job. I haven't said anything to the press and I'm not working for the Mitchell campaign."

"What about the reporter you brought along with you?"

"I just want everything that McKinley says tonight to be fair and honest."

She shook her head, then walked back and talked quietly to the group.

A few minutes later the door opened and McKinley entered the room. He looked tired and his eyes were bloodshot. James Carberry was right behind him. The crowd turned and began to applaud. McKinley smiled and held up his hands. "I appreciate your being here tonight," he said. "I know you've heard a lot of things in the news." He hesitated, then flashed another award-winning smile.

Meg motioned with her head toward me. McKinley turned, the smile momentarily frozen on his face, then he frowned.

"What's he doing here?"

"Let's go into your office and I'll explain," Carberry said putting his arm on McKinley's shoulder and trying to lead him inside.

Aaron picked that moment to enter the room. He walked over and stood next to me.

"You're a reporter," McKinley said. "Get them both the hell out of here."

Carberry leaned close to McKinley's ear and whispered, but in the silence of the office his voice sounded loud. "I thought you could talk to him before you went to your press conference."

"I've already made up my mind. Nothing will change that."

Carberry held up his hand to me, then walked over. "Give me a minute. He'll see you."

"I don't think so," I said.

"Five minutes," he said. "That's all I ask."

I focused on McKinley. He picked up the mail from the desk and flipped through it as if he didn't have a care in the world. Then he put it back down and looked at the box.

"Where'd this come from?" he said to Meg.

"Federal Express brought it. I signed. I thought you were expecting it." She smiled. "It's addressed to Governor McKinley."

McKinley's body stiffened. "When a package like this arrives put it inside on my desk."

"Yes, sir. Would you like me to do that now?"

"No." He picked it up and moved inside the office. Carberry followed him in and closed the door.

"You think he'll meet with us?" Aaron said.

"I don't know" I said. "Let's give him the five minutes."

"I need another cigarette. If he wants to meet, come and get me."

A few minutes later McKinley walked out of the office. His face was ashen. Carberry was right behind him. The people in the room turned to face him. No one said a word. If he was aware I was still there, he didn't acknowledge it.

Carberry's gaze darted around the room. "You're making a mistake, Ed," he said.

McKinley took a deep breath. "I just want to reiterate how much I appreciate the work you have all done." He hesitated as if at a loss for words. "I've spent the day with my family. The rumors you've heard are true. Susan Oliver and I did have an affair. I was only with her twice, but that's not the point. I'm sorry for the hurt I've caused everyone. I hope you will find it in your heart to forgive me. I thought you should know before I tell the press." He turned, walked into his office and shut the door.

For a few seconds no one said a word. Then Meg said, "Jim, is he dropping out of the race?"

Carberry shrugged. "I don't think he has a choice." He turned, walked toward me and leaned close to my ear. "I didn't know," he said.

I studied him for a few seconds. "What made him change his mind? Sunday he was saying he was innocent."

"Something happened. He's not telling me what. All he said was he had to tell people."

"Did the police show him the video?"

"What video?"

"The one of Susan."

Carberry looked at the workers, then motioned me outside. I followed. Aaron was across the street puffing on a cigarette. He started moving toward us. I held up my hand and he stopped. "A few minutes," I said.

We walked a few feet away from headquarters and stood in front of the jewelers. "Susan made a video accusing McKinley of fathering her child. Is that why he admitted to this?"

His face turned white. "Jesus. Where'd you hear that?"

"It doesn't matter."

"But that's impossible. Ed..."

The explosion was so loud it shook the entire block. It knocked me forward, banging me into the side of the building. It was an ear shattering sound, so close it sucked the air out of me. My vision blurred and when I looked down Carberry was lying at my feet. I looked to my left. Glass had been blown out of the McKinley headquarters window and pieces lined the sidewalk. Flames were streaking skyward. I heard the low sound of people moaning and then a loud shriek sounding over the hissing of the flames.

CHAPTER 18

I put my hand under Carberry's arm and lifted him to his feet. He closed his eyes and shook his head as if trying to clear it. Then his eyes widened and his legs wobbled. He staggered toward the door of the headquarters.

"Jesus," I yelled. "What the hell are you doing?" I moved toward him. "You can't go in there."

Carberry stopped. His body became rigid and he looked at me as if trying to figure out what had happened. Fiery pieces of debris littered the sidewalk around him. People inside groaned and called for help. A spark hissed and a car caught fire. Flames quickly engulfed it. Carberry looked at it for a second, then put his hands in front of his face and went inside.

"Damn it," I said. Broken glass crunched under my feet as I ran. Thick black smoke poured out of the doorway and seemed to cover everything.

A man stumbled out, bumping into me. He coughed, then gasped for air. "Ed's inside," he said. "We've got to help him."

I felt a sense of panic, but I knew what I had to do. I took a deep breath, put my hand over my mouth and went in. The first thing that hit me was the heat. Then an overpowering stench made my stomach flip. It was a mixture of burning wood and the smell of charred flesh.

Tables were upended and flames shot to the ceiling. Smoke burned my eyes and I shielded them with my hand trying to see. A loud shriek sounded from the corner. Carberry was helping Meg to her feet. Blood trickled from her mouth. She staggered and started to fall. Carberry struggled to keep her upright.

He looked toward me. "Help her outside. I've got to get Ed."

I pushed through the flames. "No," I said. My voice was raspy from the smoke. "We've got to get out of here. There could be another explosion."

I put my arms around Meg, struggling to keep her upright. The heat scorched my skin and I began to cough. I looked toward McKinley's office. The walls had been knocked down. If he were inside he couldn't have survived.

Carberry let go of Meg's body and her weight almost caused me to fall. He turned toward the office.

"Don't be stupid," I said. "Let's get Meg out of here."

"I can't," he said. Then he stepped over the fallen walls and into what had been the office. Through the smoke and flames I lost sight of him.

Meg coughed and gasped for air. "Help Ed," she said, but I couldn't. I just wanted to get away from the heat. I put my hand under her shoulder, stepped around the flames and took her outside. The crowd moved aside as I led her across the street. I rested my hand on her back as she bent forward and took long gasps of air.

Two policemen waved their hands at the people who watched. The people moved away. Sirens sounded in the distance and I could see two police cars speeding up the street.

A fire truck roared around a curve and came to a stop. Four firemen leaped out and began to hose down the cars. A second truck was close behind. The men raced into the headquarters.

More people streamed out of the surrounding buildings, lined the sidewalk and stared.

"It's McKinley Headquarters."

"He was inside."

"No one could survive that blast."

Within minutes McKinley's name had circulated through the crowd. Some were certain he was dead. Others claimed they had seen him get out. Then a second car caught fire and they started to scream and move away.

Meg slid to the sidewalk. Her breathing was growing more irregular. The blonde woman I had talked to inside moved beside me. Her blouse was torn and tears streamed down her face. "Meg," she said.

I looked toward the burning building. Carberry hadn't come out. I pushed through the crowd and headed toward the doorway. A fireman blocked my way. "Anyone still inside?" he said.

"At least two."

The fireman turned and went in.

I wanted to follow, but the heat drove me back. I felt both nauseated and helpless.

Water cascaded off the front of the building. I saw Aaron looking at the smoke which billowed through the broken windows. An ambulance pulled to the front and stopped. Sirens sounded and I saw more ambulances approaching.

Carberry walked slowly out of the building. His face was blackened by soot and he was struggling to breathe. He said something to a policeman, then closed his eyes and braced himself against a wall, breathing deeply.

Aaron moved beside me. "You heard anything about McKinley."

I shook my head.

Aaron stretched his neck. "There's Carberry. I got to talk to him."

Two cops moved toward us. "Okay, folks. Go about your business and let us do ours."

Carberry got into a cruiser. I watched as it pulled away from the curb.

"I'm gonna stay here," Aaron said. "You can take my car if you want to leave. I can hitch a ride later." He flipped me his keys and walked into the crowd.

I stared at the flames and watched as the firemen and cops did their jobs. I don't know how long I stood there. It seemed more like a movie than reality. The horror of it hadn't sunk in yet. I closed my eyes for a few seconds. When I opened them the flames and devastation hadn't gone away. I starting walking. I needed to get away from it. I don't know how I got to Aaron's car. I don't remember the streets I crossed or the route I took. I made a U-turn and stepped hard on the accelerator. Then I flipped on the radio. The details reporters gave were sketchy. No one seemed to know about McKinley.

When I got home I took a shower and let the hot water pour over my body. I scrubbed my skin until it was raw, as if that would wash away the stench.

Ten minutes later I was sitting on my couch watching the television reports. Channel Four had reporters at McKinley headquarters, thc Park Plaza and Bcth Israel Hospital where it was rumored McKinley had been taken. Eyewitnesses told of the devastation.

I turned the volume down and picked up the phone. Beth had been sleeping. I heard it in her voice when she answered.

"It's Steve. I'm sorry to wake you."

"That's all right," she said. "What time is it? God it's only ten. I must have dozed off."

"I'm sorry."

She hesitated. "Is everything okay?"

"Did you listen to the news tonight?"

"No. I was painting for awhile and then I lay down on the couch to read. I must have fallen asleep. Why?"

"There's been a bombing at McKinley headquarters. He might have been killed. No one knows yet. I was there."

"Are you all right?"

On TV a reporter was standing in front of the Park Plaza. He squinted and shook his head. I wondered how much emotion he was really feeling.

"Steve?"

"No. I'm not all right. I feel like everything is coming apart around me. First Susan, then someone takes a shot at me and now this. I called you because you're the only one I could think of who would understand. I could have been in that room. I could have been killed."

"Come over."

Fifteen minutes later I was sitting on Beth's couch. The television murmured in the background, but I didn't pay any attention. I talked for a long time. I rambled all over the place, from the beginning to what happened tonight. A lot of it she already knew, but she listened anyway. I had to get it in perspective, sort it out in my mind and hope it made some kind of sense.

She got up and brought me a glass of water. I kept right on talking as if she was in the room. "I didn't know what the hell to do. The explosion happened and I wanted to rush inside, but at first I wasn't thinking straight and then the heat drove me back. People were moaning. Blood seemed to be everywhere and I couldn't do anything about it. I felt like I was losing it."

She handed me the water. "You did right by coming here."

"Shit, when McKinley admitted to the affair I thought that bastard killed Susan. It all made sense. Now someone tries to blow him away. It's gotta be connected. So who killed Susan?"

"The police will find out."

I shook my head. "I'm not so sure. Someone's setting me up. First I find Susan's body. Then someone lets Aaron see her diary and it's full of lies. Why would she do that? And now McKinley. Someone wants it to look like I'm guilty. Question is how far are they willing to go?"

Beth rubbed my neck. "Get some sleep, honey. When you wake up maybe things will make more sense."

I took a long gulp of water, put my head back and closed my eyes. My thoughts jumped all over the place. At one point I realized I was talking about myself. Telling Beth things I never said before. My whole life seemed to spill out of me as I watched the flickering images on the screen. I talked about how much I hated being an only child, how overprotective my mother became when my father died, how I rebelled by acting out in school and how two years in the army changed me and why I became a teacher. I told her how our divorce had affected me, how I relived what I should have done and what I should have said. How I thought I had failed her.

She remained quiet, her eyes focused on me. At that point I didn't want her to say anything. I just wanted her there.

The eleven o'clock news came on and stayed with the McKinley story. My eyes were focused on the screen, but I wasn't really hearing what was being said.

Susan Oliver had been killed.

Edward McKinley had had an affair with her.

Someone had tried to kill him.

These things had to be connected and I was being pulled in.

When James Carberry came on the screen I quickly turned up the volume.

He still had soot on his cheeks. I knew what he was going to say before he spoke. "Edward McKinley was pronounced dead at ten-fifteen p.m. At his side were his wife and their three children. Any questions should be directed to the doctors, who tried valiantly to save Ed's life. They will be speaking to you shortly."

"Any idea who might have done this?" a reporter yelled.

Carberry waved off the question. "The police are looking into that. Right now they say they have a good lead. They expect to make an arrest shortly."

We watched for a few more minutes, then Beth flipped off the television. I stared at the blank screen for awhile before I realized she had her arm draped over my shoulder. "Why don't you try and get some rest," she said. "You can sleep on the couch."

I tossed and turned for awhile, then tried reading one of Beth's art books on Monet. But I couldn't concentrate. I sat in the dark by a window looking out at the street light in front of the house. It was after two before I went back to the couch.

When I woke up my head was aching. Beth must have checked on me during the night because I had a quilt covering my legs. At six she was already in the kitchen making coffee. Listening to her footsteps made me think of the days we had been married. It was six years ago. Things had seemed so much simpler then.

We didn't talk much over coffee. I felt drained and tired. Then she kissed me on the cheek and I left.

At school the talk was about McKinley. When people asked me what I thought, I just shrugged. I didn't mention I had been there.

When my first class arrived, Billy said, "You hear about that McKinley guy?"

I nodded. Usually I encouraged my students to talk about current events, but not today. I was afraid if I told them the truth they'd ask if I was a suspect in McKinley's death too. I couldn't concentrate and I'd stare off into space. My mind would flash to McKinley and I'd see the flames and hear people screaming.

Every time my classroom door opened I expected it to be the cops.

Around eleven Mr. Webster knocked on my door. He motioned me out into the hallway. "There's a policeman who wants to see you."

His eyes narrowed and I could tell by his expression that he wanted to know what it was about. When I didn't respond he said, "He's in my office. I'll watch your class till you're through."

I stopped in the conference room and called Lisa Gerrault. I explained about being at McKinley headquarters and the cop who was waiting in Webster's office. She said to give her ten minutes to get to the school.

The cop was sitting in Webster's chair and talking on the phone. He motioned me to sit. He appeared to be in his early fifties, although it was hard to judge. His skin had the brown toughness of an outdoorsman and his graying hair was cut short.

When he finished on the phone he got up and leaned on the desk a few feet from where I was sitting. "Name's Foster. You mind telling me why you were at McKinley Headquarters last night?"

"Mr. Foster. I'm willing to cooperate with you any way I can, but I'd like my lawyer present. I've already called her. She's on her way."

"Yes, sir, that's fine."

"You want some coffee. It should only take her a few minutes to get here."

He shook his head.

I left him in the office and went out into the main lobby to wait. A few minutes later Lisa arrived. She was carrying a briefcase and wearing a navy wool jacket with a gray skirt.

"Did you say anything to him?"

"Just offered him coffee. He didn't want any."

"You did right by calling me," she said as we headed toward Webster's office. "I'll stay out of things unless you start getting yourself into trouble."

Foster rose and shook hands with Lisa. Then we all sat.

"My client is willing to help you in any way he can. He is, of course, aware of his constitutional rights."

"Yes, Ma'am. Mr. Asher, do you have any objections to answering some questions?"

"He does not."

I looked at Lisa. So far she was doing a great job staying out of things.

"No, sir. I don't."

"Why were you at McKinley headquarters last night?"

"James Carberry asked me to go. I was supposed to meet with McKinley before his press conference."

"About?"

I hesitated.

"Guy's dead," he said. "I suggest you be honest with me."

I nodded, then told him about the video and what Carberry had said on the phone. Foster listened silently and occasionally wrote in a small note pad.

When I finished he said, "McKinley spent the day with his family, told them he'd had an affair and he couldn't deny it. He was going to admit his mistake and continue the campaign. Why would he want to meet with you?"

I looked at Lisa expecting her to object. Instead she nodded her head. "Carberry didn't know that. He was going to try and straighten things out."

"Carberry will verify this."

I nodded, but the truth was I didn't know what Carberry would say.

Foster stared at me for a few seconds as if he expected me to say something. "Ever been to campaign headquarters before last night?"

I nodded. "On Sunday. I wanted to find out why McKinley went to the Olivers' house on Saturday night." I explained about my meeting with him on Sunday afternoon.

"Some of his staff said you had it in for him. One said you tried to pass yourself off as a campaign worker on Sunday. Another one said you leaked stories to the press."

"None of that's true," I said. "The story is exactly what I told you."

"You're a suspect in the Oliver murder. Woman wrote in her diary you two were dating and you deny it. Now your name comes up again and you're saying McKinley's staff is lying. Kinda funny, don't you think?"

I looked at Lisa. Her eyes were locked on Foster's. "I can't explain things any better than I did," I said.

He wrote a few more things in his note pad, then closed it. "I'm gonna want to talk to you again."

"My client will be glad to answer any further questions which are relevant to your investigation."

When Foster left the office I turned to Lisa. "Jesus, I expected a little more help from you than that."

"Why? You did fine. Guy was on a fishing expedition. They don't have any hard evidence in either killing, but the minute they think they have a real case, they'll come for you and, believe me, they're going to work like hell to build one."

On the way back to my class I went into the men's room and splashed water on my face. In the mirror I could see dark black circles under my eyes. I felt drained and exhausted. Foster's questions had rattled me. The last thing the school committee needed to hear was I had been questioned in connection with the McKinley murder.

At the end of the day I went home. I just wanted to sleep. Maybe that would help me to see things clearly. As I pulled into my driveway I noted that Aaron's car was gone. Dave was looking out his window. I walked into the hallway just as he came out of his apartment.

"A damn shame about McKinley." He hesitated as if waiting for a response. When I didn't say anything, he continued. "Cop was here today looking for you. Told me you were at McKinley headquarters when it happened. I told him you were at school. Did he show up?"

I nodded and told Dave how I had ended up at McKinley's. "Then I went over to Beth's."

"That's what I figured. You want to talk about it?"

I shook my head.

Dave squinted and he began to rub his arm. From his expression I could tell something was bothering him. "What's wrong?" I said.

"Nothing. Everything's fine."

"I know you well enough to know when something's bothering you. Why don't you just tell me?"

"I didn't want to mention it because it's probably nothing." He hesitated. "There's been a strange car driving by all day."

I smiled. By "strange" Dave usually meant a car owned by anyone who didn't live in the neighborhood.

"It went by five times. It'd slow down like it was checking out the place and then drive away. With the break-ins and everything I figured I better call the police. I wanted to get the plate number for them, but I haven't seen the car since."

"What kind of car was it?"

"You know I'm not good with cars. It was a dark blue sedan and new. I know it was new."

"Probably reporters wanting to talk to me," I said. "Or maybe the police in an unmarked car waiting for me to get home."

"Yeah, that must be it," he said. "The Waltham police didn't seem too concerned."

"It couldn't be burglars. They don't usually drive by a place five times in the daytime if they're casing it," I said. "Look I gotta get some sleep."

There were no messages on my machine. I checked Richard's food and water before going into the living room. I sat on a chair by the window and looked out into the street. The more I thought about the car continually driving by the house, the stranger it seemed. I ran through possibilities in my mind of who it might be. I went over and double-checked the lock on the door, then stretched out on the couch.

I was just starting to doze when the doorbell rang and there was a loud banging on my door.

"Steve." It was Dave. "It's that car again. It just went by the house. It stopped at the end of the street."

I ran down the stairs. Dave was out in the street staring into the distance. I followed his gaze. A dark blue Chevy was stopped at the end.

"It went by too fast. I couldn't get the license number."

The anger that I felt last night came pouring back. I jumped into my car and backed out of the driveway just as the Chevy disappeared around the corner.

CHAPTER 19

I drove to the end of the street just as the Chevy rounded a corner. I stepped on the gas and followed it out onto Main Street. I wanted to get close enough to see his plate number. When he drove by City Hall I got caught at a light. He took a left. After the light changed I followed. The car had slowed as if it was waiting for me, then picked up speed.

I had a feeling he was leading me somewhere and when the car took a right I knew where. We were only two blocks from Petey's house. A few minutes later he turned onto the Olivers' street and picked up speed. His tires squealed as he rounded the curve after the Olivers. I followed and he pulled back onto Main. He must have been doing sixty. Where the hell was a cop when you needed one? I swerved around a car as I went through a red light. Horns blared and a car cut in front of me and slowed. When I was able to pass he was gone. I drove around for awhile, but saw no sign of him.

There had to be a reason the driver had led me to the Olivers. I made a U-Turn and five minutes later I was parked in front of Petey's house.

I studied the house for a few seconds. I had wanted to talk to Mrs. Oliver anyway to find out if she knew why Susan would lie about me in her diary. Maybe she'd know something about the driver who had led me here. I got out of my car and walked slowly up the front steps.

A light was on in the living room, but the curtains were pulled and I couldn't see inside. I looked at my watch. Six p.m. The sound of a car door slamming made me turn. A heavy set muscular man got out of a black Ford and started walking quickly toward me. He appeared to be in his mid-forties. His hair was cut short, military-style and he had on a light gray sport jacket. He looked like a cop.

"Hold up," he said. "What business you got here?"

"I'm Petey's teacher. I'm here to see how he's doing."

"He's doing fine."

"You a cop?" I said.

The man looked me over, but didn't respond. There was a bulge under the arm of his sport jacket.

"You see a dark, blue Chevy go by?" I said.

He nodded. "And I saw you go right after him. What's it all about?"

""'I'm not sure. Have you seen the car before?"

He shook his head.

"Is it okay if I go in and talk to Petey?"

He took a step in my direction. He outweighed me by about forty pounds and was a good six inches taller. "No," he said.

I shrugged. "How about if we both go in together?"

He put his hand on my shoulder. "How about if you turn around and go home."

I smiled. "In college I had a choice whether to take a course in bowling or boxing. I chose bowling. Maybe if I had a bowling ball we'd be even."

He narrowed his eyes and they locked on mine.

"You trying to hypnotize me," I said. "That would be good. Maybe you could help me cut down on my eating."

The front door opened and Mrs. Oliver stepped out on the porch. I almost didn't recognize her. She wore heavy make-up which did little to camouflage the dark circles under her eyes, but changed her appearance. She looked older and more haggard then she had at the funeral. "What's going on, Ben?"

"Nothing. This guy was just leaving."

"It's Steve Asher, Mrs. Oliver."

I could tell by her expression she wasn't happy to see me. "It's all right, Ben," she said. Then she opened the screen door and motioned me inside.

I gave Ben a wink and followed.

"Please leave the door open," she said, as I entered.

A narrow hallway led into the living room. The room was small and crowded. She motioned me toward a couch that sagged in the middle, then switched off the TV and sat in a chair opposite me.

She had on beige slacks and a pale yellow sweater. On the mantle was a picture of Susan with her arm draped around Petey's shoulder. They were both smiling. There were no pictures of Cynthia.

"The cops keeping an eye on the house?" I said motioning toward the street.

Her eyes flickered. "A private detective."

I waited for her to say more. When she didn't, I said, "That's a good idea, but it must be pretty expensive."

A trace of a smile passed her lips. "We'll manage."

"A '92 dark blue Chevy just led me on a chase right to your door. You wouldn't know anything about it?"

She looked away for a few seconds. Then shook her head. "That's very strange. You say it led you here?"

I nodded. "Must be a reason for it."

Her body became rigid. "Why are you here, Mr. Asher?"

"I was wondering how Petey is."

"He's asleep. Been real tired lately. We all have."

I looked down a narrow hallway. A door with a Larry Bird poster on it was open. Mrs. Oliver followed my gaze.

"I really couldn't disturb him now, but I'll tell him you dropped by." She got up and started for the door as if dismissing me.

"How are you doing?" I said.

"Good, good. Friends have been dropping by and Cynthia's been a big help. I don't mean to be rude, but I am very tired."

I got up. "I understand. If there's anything I can do."

"No. No. Cynthia's gonna stay around till after Thanksgiving, but then she has to go back to New York. Got a part in a play. We all hope it will be her big break."

I walked toward the door, then turned. "Mrs. Oliver, I have to ask you this. Susan and I never dated, yet she wrote in her diary that we did. I'm trying to figure out why. Is there anything you can tell me?"

Her shoulders sagged. "Susan was special. The one I depended on." She closed her eyes and sighed. "It's hard to believe she won't be walking through that door anymore."

"I'm sorry. Maybe I shouldn't have brought it up, but if we knew why she lied it might help the cops find her killer."

"My daughter didn't lie." Her words were clipped as she emphasized each one.

"The cops consider me a suspect based on what she wrote. You don't think I killed Susan or you wouldn't have let me into the house."

She smiled. It made me feel uneasy. "Ben's right outside."

"I know. If you didn't come out he was going to pick me up by the back of my neck and deposit me in my car like I was a kitten." I paused. "Mrs. Oliver. I'm just trying to help."

Her face reddened. "That bastard had no right to print Susan's private thoughts in the paper. It sickened me. I only let the police have it because I thought it might help them find Susan's killer."

"So who let Fleming see Susan's diary? Could Cynthia have shown it to him?"

She shook her head. "She was as disgusted as I was."

"Who else could have shown it to him?"

"I've already asked you to leave. Don't make me call Ben."

The phone book listed a Franklin family at 37 Brewster Street, two blocks from where the Olivers lived. Molly Franklin was Susan's best friend. Maybe she'd know about Susan's diary.

Her house was a brown two-story. The red shutters looked like they had been recently painted. The front porch sagged in the middle and the neighborhood could have used some cleaning up.

I climbed the steps and rang the doorbell. The man who opened the door frowned. The white tee shirt he wore barely covered his paunch.

"Is Molly at home?" I said.

He shook his head. "Anything I can do for you?"

"I don't think so. I was a friend of Susan Oliver."

"Terrible tragedy. Makes you appreciate what you have."

"Yes sir, it does. I'm a teacher at the middle school. I work with kids every day. Susan's brother is one of my students."

His shoulders relaxed and he smiled. "Molly's probably down at The Chateau having a drink with some of her friends."

The lounge at The Chateau was attached to an Italian restaurant. The lights were dim and the place reeked of stale smoke. Keno screens were on the wall and a few people sitting at tables played. It wasn't crowded on this Thursday night. Molly was smoking a cigarette and sipping a beer at the bar with another woman. Neither looked up when I came in.

I sat a few stools down and ordered a beer. Molly looked about Susan's age with dark brown hair. She wore a black wrap-around skirt and a red sweater. She crushed her cigarette in the ash tray. I picked up my drink and moved to the stool next to her. "Molly," I said.

When she swiveled toward me her eyes narrowed. I could tell she didn't recognize me at first. Then she frowned. "Oh. It's you."

"I just came from the Olivers. They have a private detective watching the house. It gave me an uneasy feeling. I don't want to see anything happen to the family."

"How'd you know I was here?"

"Your father told me. I said I was a teacher. That usually convinces people I'm harmless."

She smiled quickly. The bartender asked if she wanted another beer. She nodded. "Put it on his tab," she said, pointing at me. "So you came looking for me. Why?"

"I didn't date Susan. I'm trying to find out why she said we did. Maybe it'll help the police find her killer."

"I don't see how it could, and anyway, I got nothing to say to you."

"Just tell me about Susan. Maybe it'll remind you of something. Maybe it'll help me to understand her. I don't know. I just know I want Susan's murderer caught as much as you do. What have you got to lose?"

"I already talked to the police. I'm surprised they haven't picked you up."

"They haven't arrested me because I didn't do it. I just tried to see Petey and his mother said he was sleeping. I didn't think she was telling the truth. She didn't want me to talk to him, but I can't figure out why."

She stared at me for a few seconds then swiveled and whispered something in the other woman's ear. She grabbed her beer, a bowl of pretzels and motioned me to a corner table.

When we sat down she said, "You know who you remind me of?"

"Lassie?"

"The guy in all those Die Hard movies."

"Bruce Willis."

"Yeah. That's him. You got the same eyes."

I nodded. "Actually those Die Hard movies are based on my life."

She raised her hand and held it about two inches from the side of my head. "Did you know you got a crimson aura?"

"People tell me that all the time."

She popped a pretzel into her mouth and studied me. "It means you're adventurous."

I nodded. "That's true. Sometimes I don't clap the blackboard erasers at school for three or four days."

"Let me see your hand."

I held it out and she ran her finger along a line on my palm.

"That tickles."

"That's your lifeline. It's long, but there's a break in it right here."

"What does that mean? Did I die in 1985 and no one told me?"

She let go of my hand. "Is everything a joke with you?"

"Finding Susan's body wasn't."

The door opened and two men walked in. Molly watched as they sat at the bar. "Maybe you're right," she said. "Maybe talking about Susan will make me think of something that might help the police." She took a long sip of her beer. "You wanted to know what Susan was like?" She wiped her mouth with the back of her hand. "A few years ago this jerk I was dating got me pregnant. Soon as I told him he left. I'll spare you the details, but I had an abortion. Susan stayed with me every day. Made sure I ate, had someone to talk to and didn't get more depressed. She didn't tell me I'd get over it or that it was for the best. She just listened and held me. It didn't matter that I said the same things over and over. She accepted my anger and didn't desert me." Her eyes narrowed. "She didn't lie about people."

"You make her sound like a saint."

"We were lovers for awhile. Does that shock you, teach?"

"Believe it or not, most teachers have entered the twentieth century."

She stared at me for a few seconds. "You were her mystery man. She only told a few of us, and she wasn't bragging. Said she loved you. That's something she'd never said before, not even when she married Damon. She told me you got her pregnant and that you two were gonna get married. Susan wouldn't lie to me about something like that. That's what I told the cops."

I drummed my fingers on the table. "It's all bullshit."

Molly shook her head. "She told me she was never going to have to worry about money again."

"I'm a teacher for Chrissake. No one marries a teacher to get rich."

She shrugged and took another sip of beer. "That's what she said and Susan really cared about money. Not necessarily for herself, but the family didn't have much. She wanted it for them."

I thought about the private detective at the Oliver house. "Did Susan make up stories very often?"

Molly smiled. "You don't give up, do you? Susan was complex. There was a side of her she didn't want anyone to see. She'd disappear for weekends and then didn't want to talk about where she was. But she wouldn't lie. That's why we got along so well. I'm complex, too. I could understand her."

"Did she have any enemies? Someone who might have wanted to kill her?"

She shook her head. "Susan had a way of making people like her—even when she'd done them wrong. Only person she truly hated was her father and she hadn't heard from him in four years."

"Did she ever mention McKinley?"

"Not to me. You got a cigarette?"

"No."

Molly looked toward her friend at the bar. "Cigarette," she said. The woman shook her head.

"McKinley admitted they had an affair."

"They might have. Susan liked casual affairs. One-nighters excited her."

"Did you tell that to the police?"

She laughed. "No. I was saving that for the tabloids." She got up. "I've gotta go pee."

"I'll just sit here with my crimson aura till you get back."

When she returned her eyes looked like slits. I suspected she'd taken something in the bathroom. We talked for awhile longer, but Molly didn't tell me anything about Susan I didn't already know. When she started talking about E.S.P, I knew it was time to leave.

Molly hadn't shed any light on why Susan lied about me in her diary. I wondered if there was something she hadn't told me. I shook my head. I'm usually a good reader of people. I felt she had told me the truth.

Everyone I talked to said the same thing about Susan. She wouldn't lie. She was a great daughter, friend, wife and lover. I kept peeling layers only to find other layers hidden inside. Where was the core? Who was the real Susan in all of this? Why would this woman lie about me in her diary and who would want to kill her?

The lights were off at Dave's when I got home. He must have gone over to Mildred's.

I turned on the television and tried to watch a movie with Cary Grant. What I really needed was a football game where the tackles thudded so hard the TV set shook. Instead all I got was Cary hiring Sophia Loren to take care of his three kids while they all tried to live on a houseboat.

Cary's whining started to get on my nerves. I shut off the TV and sat in the dark by the window looking out at the street lights.

It must have been ten when the phone rang. I let the machine pick it up.

"Mr. Asher." It was Petey.

I grabbed the phone. "I tried to see you earlier," I said.

He didn't answer right away. I heard the sound of traffic whooshing in the background. "Where are you calling from?"

"It doesn't matter. I left for good this time. Don't worry about me. I'll be fine." He hung up.

I stared at the phone for a few seconds then dialed Rita Dooley's house. "I just walked in the door, Steve. What's up?"

"Petey just called me. Said he's taken off again. Wouldn't say where he was."

"Jesus," she said. "Let me check on it. I'll call you right back."

I put my head back, closed my eyes and sat with the lights off. A few minutes later the phone rang. "No one's reported it. A cruiser's gonna pick me up and we're going over." She hung up before I could respond.

I paced around the apartment. What the hell would make him run off this time? Fifteen minutes later I couldn't wait any longer. I got into my car and headed toward the Olivers.

The cruiser was just pulling away from the house when I rounded the corner. I honked, and pulled behind it. Rita got out and approached my car. "I was just on my way to see you. You sure it was Petey?"

"I'm sure."

"According to Mrs. Oliver he's in his room asleep. She wouldn't let us in, but she went and checked. Said he was there, all right."

CHAPTER 20

"I could hear traffic in the background when he called."
Rita nodded. "How'd he sound?"
"Confused, but he said he was fine."
"Maybe someone was forcing him to say that."
"Why would he call me in the first place?"
Rita looked toward the house. "She's gotta know where he is. We can't do anything official unless they report him missing."
"I didn't think Petey was home when I visited earlier." I told Rita about the car chase and my conversation with Mrs. Oliver. Then I turned toward the cars parked in front of the house. The detective they hired was sitting in one. "Did you talk to him?" I said pointing toward his car.
"Yeah. Claims no one came to the house. As far as he knows Petey's still inside."
"Maybe he went off with Cynthia. She could have taken him out the back way"
"She's home. Told us we should be looking for Susan's murderer and not bothering the family."
"Let's go, Dooley," Hollowell yelled from the car.
"Just a sec," she said. "Steve, I can't force them to let us in to look around."
"So what can you do?"
"Make a few phone calls. Tell people to keep their eyes open. That's about it for now. I'm working tomorrow night so I can do some looking on my own during the day."
I watched the cruiser pull away. Then I drove around for awhile hoping I might see Petey. I circled by the Olivers again. The lights were on and the curtains closed tight. The detective was still sitting in front of the house. "Where the hell are you, Petey?" I said aloud.

The message light on my machine was flashing. Aaron wanted me to call him. "What's up," I said.

"Rumor has it the police are about to make an arrest in the McKinley killing. Have they been around to question you?"

"Once."

"So you haven't heard anything. Shit, I'd love to track this down before the police make it public."

"You're really enjoying this, aren't you?"

"Give me a break, will ya? Four years at U-Mass majoring in journalism. Get a job on the Trib right out of college. I'm on my way, right? Seven years later I'm still covering school committee meetings and flower shows. You've got to make your own luck. A big story like this is what I've dreamt about. I'll investigate every nook until I find out who killed McKinley."

"You're not an investigative reporter," I said. "So watch yourself."

"Don't worry. I can handle myself."

I thought of Aaron's fragile frame and shook my head. "Let me know if you hear anything."

"Will do." He hung up.

I flipped on the TV and sat with the sound low. I was glad I didn't tell Aaron about Petey's phone call. I wasn't sure what he'd do with the information. He'd probably hear the rumor soon enough.

The eleven o'clock news came on and a familiar face flashed on the screen. Her haircut was new, shorter, almost spiked, which is why I couldn't place her at first. Then I recognized Lois McKinley. I turned the volume up.

She was seated in a large armchair being questioned by a reporter. A smiling picture of the family was on a table behind her. She talked about what a wonderful man Ed had been and the senselessness of his murder. She seemed composed for a woman who'd just lost her husband. When the reporter asked about Susan Oliver I sat up straighter. "Ed had no involvement with that woman at all. That's one thing I'm sure about. Rumors were being spread to try and sabotage the campaign and destroy our family. Yesterday Ed explained everything to me and the children. She had stalked him. She wanted money, or else she was going to spread lies about an affair. Someone else was involved and Ed knew who it was."

"Did he tell you who was involved?"

"I've told everything I know to the police."

"Do you think that person might have killed your husband?"

"The police are looking into it."

The interview lasted another few minutes, but my mind wandered. McKinley had admitted to the affair the last time I had seen him. Lois McKinley seemed intent on saving her husband's reputation. I wondered how long it would be before the real story came out.

When I woke on Friday morning a wet snow was falling. I scrambled a couple of eggs, added some hot pepper, chili sauce and sliced up an onion. I read the Globe while I ate. The police were still following leads in the McKinley murder. There was no mention of a connection between him and Susan Oliver.

The snow was sticking to the grass but not the roadway. Not enough to call off school. I checked Richard's food and water. "First snow of the season," I said. "Maybe I'll buy you a pair of ear muffs for Christmas."

I stopped off at the Sacred Heart on my way to school and sat in the solitude for about ten minutes. When I got to school there was a message in my mailbox from Mr. Webster. He wanted to see me before I went to my classroom. He was sitting at his desk when I entered the office.

"Shut the door," he said, then motioned for me to sit down. "The school committee has called a special meeting for Monday night to talk about your situation. My guess is you'll be suspended pending the results of the investigation. I thought you should know."

"They're making a mistake."

"Some of the members have already made up their minds. They're concerned about what they're hearing and the disruption it's causing at school. It'll only be temporary. Till things get straightened out."

"I'm bringing my lawyer to the meeting."

Webster's eyes narrowed. "I have the power to fire you."

"Yes, you do, but not without probable cause. You want to tell me exactly what it is I've done?" I waited a few seconds. When he didn't say anything I left.

I had a headache when I got to my classroom. I spent some time organizing my lessons, but had trouble focusing. I taught my first two classes trying not to take my personal problems into the classroom. It didn't work. I was short-tempered and impatient.

Sally Jensen, the guidance counselor, knocked on my door around ten o'clock and motioned me out into the hallway.

"I just heard it on the radio," she said. "The Boston police have arrested Susan's ex-husband and charged him with the murder of McKinley.

"Jesus," I said. "Did they say what evidence they had?"

She shook her head. "They're going to hold a press conference later."

"Did they mention Susan's murder."

"Not a thing."

I thought about what Damon had said at the funeral home. "If you're involved I won't wait for the police. I'll kill you myself." Thing was, as far as I knew, when the bomb went off, McKinley's involvement with Susan was just a rumor. He'd been denying it and was with his family all day.

"Steve, are you okay?" Sally said.

"Fine. Thanks."

At the end of the day I left school quickly and drove by Rita's to see if she was home.

She lived a couple of miles away from my apartment, but the neighborhood was different. The streets curved, the houses were spaced apart with circular driveways, swing sets and pools. It was part of her divorce settlement, and even though she rattled around in the eight rooms, she wasn't going to give it up.

She was munching a sandwich when she answered the door. "Come on in. I was going to call you."

The living room was wide with a light, beige shag rug. There were two upholstered chairs and a dark, cranberry leather couch. The walls were lined with vacation photographs. I noted a new one of Crater Lake from her trip to the northwest last summer.

"Nice," I said.

"It doesn't really show how blue it is. I got some other pictures I want to hang. I just haven't gotten around to it yet."

I sat on the couch and Rita plopped down beside me. Her tee shirt said "Waltham Police". I was aware of how tight it was and the smell of her perfume. Then I noticed the bottle of Johnny Walker on the coffee table.

Rita took a bite of her sandwich. "You hungry? Can I get you something?"

I shook my head. "Anything on Petey?" I said.

"Nothing. I made a few phone calls, did some looking on my own. The Olivers still haven't reported him missing. It doesn't make sense, but I'll keep looking around."

"Do you know anything about Damon Saulnier's arrest?"

"I talked to a cop I know in Boston. They feel they have a good case. He told me Saulnier used his credit card to buy the package he rigged the bomb to."

"Pretty dumb and real convenient for the cops."

"You'd be surprised how we crack some cases. People can be pretty stupid sometimes. Maybe he thought all the evidence would be destroyed when the bomb went off. Anyway, they also got a tip he was in the area that night. Saunier denies it. Claims someone stole his credit card."

"He threatened me at the funeral house. Said if he found out I was involved in Susan's death, he'd kill me."

"Boston cops feel it was revenge for McKinley's affair with Susan."

"Then Saulnier would have had to know before McKinley confessed," I said. "He was still denying his involvement when he was killed."

She looked toward the window and didn't respond. When she turned back she looked at the scotch bottle.

"What's wrong?" I said.

"Most of the time I love this job. I really do. But sometimes things get to you. Things you try not to think about and every once in awhile you have to get it out of your system."

"You want to talk about it?"

"We've been friends for a long time, Steve. I value that friendship." She hesitated. "The investigation into Susan's murder has been stopped. No one will say that officially, but that's what happened."

"I don't understand."

"The feeling is McKinley did it, but they're never gonna prove it.

Wife claims he was at home. She could be lying. If she's telling the truth he could've gotten someone to take her out. They'll never find out unless they get lucky and there's pressure to lay off the investigation."

"Pressure from who?"

"I don't know. Maybe the wife's family. They're pretty influential."

"So no one is going to look for Susan's murderer."

"The line is the case is officially open, but yeah, they're gonna let it die."

"I'm not so sure McKinley did it."

"Use your head. Susan's gonna release a tape to the media and tell about their affair. He just lost it and kills her. Then he attempts to cover it up by admitting to the affair figuring people wouldn't think he'd tell about that if he killed her."

"There's too many unexplained loose ends. Why would McKinley be at Walden with Susan? Why admit to the affair at all? He could just deny it. Say she was crazy."

"We're never gonna find out what happened. McKinley's dead and it's been a week since Susan was murdered. Nothing incriminating has turned up. Just let it go. You should be happy you're not a suspect anymore."

I shook my head. "The school committee's meeting on Monday to decide whether or not to suspend me until the investigation is over."

"I'll talk to Nash. Maybe he'll tell the committee you're not a suspect."

"I don't think he'd do it. Hell, the last time I talked to him I thought he was going to take me in." I paused. "You know what really makes me angry? Whoever killed Susan is going to get away with it. You just can't leave it like this."

"I don't have any choice. I'm not involved in the investigation. I don't know what they have. I wish I was involved because I wouldn't let things slide like this. I'd go after whoever did it."

"Shit. If Susan's killer isn't found a lot of people I know are always going to wonder if I did it. Hell, the kids I teach will wonder. The only way to change that is for the cops to get Susan's killer."

"I don't think that's possible."

I slumped back in the couch.

We talked for awhile longer, but I found myself getting angrier. I didn't want to take it out on Rita. It wasn't her fault the investigation was dropped.

When I left her house my headache was worse. Maybe everything the police had did point to McKinley. Maybe his family had suffered enough and the cops were right. What bothered me was Susan's family didn't have the influence to keep the investigation going.

I stopped at Brennen's pub, sat at the bar, ordered a Heineken and a bacon cheeseburger. I watched the news at six and saw Damon Saulnier being taken to the police station in handcuffs. Police said they had a strong case against him, but weren't saying what it was. The reporter speculated on the motive. Saulnier's lawyer said his client didn't do it. Everyone in the bar seemed to have an opinion on the murder and most wanted to talk about it.

I ordered another beer and by the time I left, Wheel of Fortune was on and it was close to seven-thirty. When I pulled into my yard Dave's car was gone and I remembered he had driven to the Cape to visit his daughter. He wouldn't be back until late tonight.

Richard cackled a greeting as I entered. I tapped my finger against his cage. He cocked his head. "God, you need a haircut," I said.

I flipped the lights on in the living room and that's when I knew something was wrong. Several compact discs were scattered on the coffee table as if someone had looked through them. I had put them away last night. Then I noticed the player was on.

I quickly walked through the rest of the house. Whoever had gotten in hadn't broken the lock. Nothing seemed missing and the only thing that was touched were the compact discs. I thought of the Chevy that led me to the Olivers. Someone had gotten into my apartment and they wanted me to know it.

I dialed nine-one-one. Maybe I'd sound silly telling the cops someone moved my compact discs around, but I wanted them here. Hell, I wanted a cruiser sitting on the street watching the house.

I went into the bedroom to change my shirt. Maybe I'd pack a few things and stay downstairs with Dave. When I opened the closet door what I saw didn't register at first. All of my clothes had been tossed on the floor. In their place was another wardrobe and it wasn't mine. I thumbed through the strange suits and shirts. It didn't make sense. If someone was trying to drive me crazy it was beginning to work.

I sat on the bed and stared at the clothes. I noticed a western shirt. Then I glanced at the cowboy boots on the floor. "Jesus," I said. "He wore those on Sunday."

The clothes belonged to Edward McKinley.

CHAPTER 21

My first instinct was to get out of the apartment and wait for the cops. This was the fourth break-in at my place, but it spooked me the most. Instead I went into the living room, sat on the couch and tried not to keep staring at the clock.

When Rita and Hollowell arrived I explained what I had found. They looked at one another for an instant. Then I led them into the bedroom and showed them the clothes.

"Did you touch them?" Hollowell said.

"No. I studied them. Didn't recognize them at first. Then I saw the western shirt and boots. He was wearing them once when I met him."

"Did you come home right after school?" Rita said.

I looked at her. Maybe she didn't want to mention that I was at her place in front of Hollowell. "I went to Brennan's. Didn't get in until about thirty minutes ago. Dave's been at the Cape all day so no one's been home. I didn't see any sign of forced entry. Guy must have been a pro."

"Maybe," Rita said.

I shook my head. "Why would someone do this? What's the point?"

"I don't know," Rita said. "Not yet. Not for certain."

"You got a theory?"

"Guy's organized, confident and wants to play with us, but no, I don't know why he did this."

Hollowell left the bedroom and went into the kitchen. Rita pushed back her hair and looked around the bedroom. Her eyes locked on one of Beth's paintings.

"There must have been a break-in at McKinley's," I said.

"We're gonna check."

I could hear Hollowell talking softly on the telephone.

"Someone's showing off," I said. "Being clever. Doesn't make sense though, does it?"

"No. We'll talk with the neighbors. This one was done in daylight. Maybe someone saw something unusual. Maybe we'll catch a break. Did you check to see if anything's missing?"

"Not real close, but it doesn't look like it."

"Why don't you. Drawers, cabinets, anyplace someone might stash things. Not now. After we've dusted the place."

I nodded. Rita turned and walked out into the kitchen, leaving me alone. She seemed different. More formal. No wisecracks. More like a cop just doing her job. I wondered if it had to do with our talk earlier. Maybe she felt she told me too much.

When I walked through the kitchen Rita was talking on the phone. She turned away from me.

"Someone put compact discs on the glass coffee table," I said to Hollowell.

He nodded, then walked toward the living room.

I went downstairs and let myself into Dave's. I sat on his couch and tried to put things together. Someone had gone to a lot of trouble. I felt they were trying to tell me something about McKinley, but I couldn't figure out what.

It was after ten when Rita knocked on Dave's door. "We're all through. We packed up McKinley's clothes and took them. If you'd make a closer check around the apartment we'd appreciate it. We contacted the Boston cops. They tried to reach Mrs. McKinley. She's not home, but they got a guy there who'll check as soon as she gets in." She paused. "Maybe someone's trying to tell us we arrested the wrong man for McKinley's murder."

"Strange way to do it. Why not just phone in a tip? Why go through the trouble of stealing his clothes and then breaking into my place. There's gotta be something else involved."

"Maybe it's some kind of message just for you."

I nodded. "Probably trying to tell me I should buy some new clothes."

She smiled, but it looked artificial.

"You okay?" I said.

"Fine."

"Look, if you're worried about what we talked about this afternoon..."

"It's more than that. It's the job. I'm not sure I want to do it anymore. The feeling's been coming on for awhile, but this Oliver thing really bothers me."

"It bothers me too. Giving up police work is a decision only you can make. I think it'd be a mistake. You're good at being a cop. You should hear the way the kids at school talk about you. Besides, who'd come to my place twice a month when someone breaks in?"

"Maybe you could hire me for a security guard."

I was about to respond when Hollowell came down the stairs. "You two gettin' cozy again?"

"You know, Hollowell," Rita said, "sometimes you can be a real asshole." She turned and walked out the door.

I went back upstairs, double-locked the door, then checked cabinets and drawers, but didn't find anything missing. When Dave came home I didn't have the energy to tell him what happened.

I tried to sleep, but kept tossing and turning. My thoughts jumped around and I kept listening for strange noises.

I woke just after seven and put on some coffee. I sipped it while reading the Globe. It was full of stories about the arrest of Damon Saulnier.

After examining the bomb site and questioning eyewitnesses, the police had received an anonymous tip which gave them probable cause to search Damon Saulnier's apartment. They found a receipt for a recently purchased video recorder which police felt the bomb was packed with. In the basement were ingredients similar to ones that could be used to make a powerful explosive.

Other stories about Saunier filled most of the front part of the paper. One told of his arrest while another, accompanied by wedding pictures, told of his troubled life. His parents had died when he was in his teens and he was raised by an aunt. His life was punctuated with drinking problems and a gambling addiction. He was thirty-two when he married twenty-year-old Susan. Eyewitnesses talked of his severe jealousy and poor treatment of Susan. The marriage lasted only six months.

There was no mention of my break-in, but I hadn't expected one. When I heard Dave moving around in his apartment I went down and knocked on his door.

He had on a gray bathrobe and his thinning hair was sticking up in the back. He squinted as if he didn't recognize me.

"You lose your glasses again?" I said.

He smiled. "Not this time. Left 'em in the kitchen. What are you doing up this early? You want some breakfast?"

"No thanks." I went inside and sat at Dave's kitchen table. He picked up his glasses and put them on.

"How's Brenda doing?" I said.

"She's finding it rough being a single parent. Her ex-husband's always late with the child-support. She's going to a shrink. Can you believe that?"

"It'll probably help," I said. "Actually I've always thought psychoanalysis was a myth kept alive by the couch industry."

"You sure you don't want some coffee. It's hazlenut."

"Okay."

Dave poured out two mugs, brought them to the table and sat down.

I took a sip and told him about the break-in and finding Edward McKinley's clothes in my closet."

Dave's mouth opened, but nothing came out for several seconds. Then he said. "The car that kept going by."

"I thought of that, but that was before McKinley got killed. I can't see any connection. It's like someone is trying to tell me something."

Dave stared off into space. "Did you check the pockets of his clothes?"

I shook my head.

Dave got up. "Let's go. Maybe the guy left a message."

I put my hand on his shoulder. "The cops already took the stuff. I'll call Rita. Make sure they check."

"Rita have any ideas?"

"She can't figure it out either."

Dave sat back down and took a sip of his coffee. Then he shook his head. "I was thinking of having Brenda and Jake come live with me awhile. Figured it might help, but I can't. Not if the neighborhood's not safe."

"I think the last two break-ins are connected to Susan's death. I just don't know how."

We finished our coffee and talked about Dave's plans to expand his back-yard garden. Then he said, "Did that Lieutenant get ahold of you."

"Nash?"

"Yeah. That's his name. He was around here yesterday morning. Looked out in the yard, then asked permission to look in your apartment. I told him he'd have to ask you."

"Did he say anything else?"

"No. He just left."

When I got back up stairs it was after eight. I wondered why Nash wanted to look around in my apartment. It went against what Rita had told me about the investigation being stopped. I called Police Headquarters. Nash wasn't in and I left a message saying it was important I talk to him.

Thirty minutes later he called.

"You wanted to get into my apartment yesterday?" I said.

"Not important. I was just trying to tie up some loose ends."

"That's funny. A friend of mine told me the Oliver murder investigation is over."

"Bullshit. I got other things on my plate now and the state police aren't giving us the manpower we need, but the investigation is ongoing."

"That's what they said you'd say."

"Actually I'm glad you called. It will save me a trip. What can you tell me about the Olivers?"

My mind flashed to Lisa Gerrault. She had said not to talk to the cops without her present. Maybe all Nash was looking for was background. "Which one?"

"All of them. Let's start with Mrs. Oliver. I know all the background stuff. I'm just interested in your gut. I don't care if it's just something you heard. Tell me and let me find out if it's true."

I gave Nash my impressions of Cynthia and Mrs. Oliver based on things Petey told me.

"What about the old man?" Nash said.

"Stopped paying child support years ago and the family's tried to locate him without any luck. Guess he had a drinking problem. That's why they split up."

"What about the brother?"

"He's dead."

"I know, but did Petey ever talk about him?"

"Never and I always thought that was strange. Guy I met in Hadley said he thought Dwight was gay. As for Susan I told you all I know, except Damon Saulnier says the family has a history of making up stories."

"Try this story on for size," Nash said. "Susan attempted suicide twice, once when she was fourteen, then sixteen. One allegation of sexual abuse against the old man. She got married to Damon Saulnier three weeks after she met him. Marriage lasted less then six months, but you talk to the family and everything was fine. You buy that?"

"No."

"Point I'm trying to make is, the Oliver investigation isn't over. It's complex, that's all, but I'm not giving up."

"You know what I think, Lieutenant? I think you're doing most of this on your own time. That's why you didn't get a search warrant to go through my place. I think you've been told to stop looking for Susan's killer." When he didn't answer, I said. "Someone broke into my place yesterday. They didn't take anything. Just put Edward McKinley's clothes in my closet."

"I know. I heard. Someone's trying to tell you something."

"You're the third person who said that."

We talked for a few minutes more. Just before he hung up, he said. "I'm going to catch that son of a bitch."

I poured another cup of coffee, took it into the living room and looked out the window. What could someone be trying to tell me? I picked up the three C D's that they left out and studied them. Why these three? Del Shannon, Dion and Marvin Gaye. I looked at the songs listed on the back for awhile and then something hit me. "Runaround Sue" by Dion could refer to Susan and "Runaway" by Del Shannon could be Petey. I studied the songs on the Marvin Gaye disc, but nothing fit into a pattern. I smiled and shook my head. I was starting to see clues everywhere.

Then the words of Marvin Gaye's "What's Going On" went through my mind. "Mother, mother," he sang. Then "Brother, brother." I got up and started to pace. Damon Saulnier had said when he first heard Susan was dead he didn't believe it. I thought he meant because of the shock. What if he meant something else. What if the Olivers had lied about another death? It was just a hunch at first, but the more I thought about it the more sense it made. I had to find out as much about Dwight's accident as I could.

Fifteen minutes later I was sitting in a chair at the Waltham Public Library running microfiche through a scanner. Five-year-old copies of the Tribune were up on the screen. I flipped quickly until I came to the summer edition.

It had happened on the Fourth of July. Sixteen year old Dwight Oliver had been out alone in a rowboat fishing in the Connecticut River. It was after two a.m. when neighbors heard splashes and someone screaming for help. The police were called and a neighbor used a motorboat to search, but all he found was a capsized boat. Dwight's father wasn't home at the time of the accident.

I pictured the cottage in Hadley. Dwight had gone to live with his father when his parents separated. I wondered which neighbor went in search of him.

I flipped to the next day's edition. A search for the body turned up nothing. Divers talked about underwater currents. Dwight's picture accompanied the story. He looked like Petey.

A few stories followed in succeeding days. Divers had stopped the search and Dwight's death was ruled accidental. I sat back and looked toward the ceiling. None of what I read told me what I needed to know, and I knew the Olivers wouldn't tell me.

I continued to look, but didn't find any subsequent stories. I put the next years Trib in and flipped to July. Maybe there'd be a mention of the accident on it's anniversary. I didn't find anything until I got to the obituary page. A three by five box near the bottom of the page said, "In memoriam. Dwight 'Chipper' Oliver. He will always be missed.

"Jesus," I said aloud. "Petey's brother is still alive."

CHAPTER 22

The man at the next machine looked over.

I put my head back and closed my eyes. It was Chipper whom I had seen at the cemetery and who had filmed Susan's video. Petey knew, or at least suspected, his brother was alive. That's why he never mentioned his death. When he saw the video, heard Susan use Chipper's name, and recognized the cabin, he had gone to Hadley to search for his brother. That would explain why the Olivers didn't report Petey missing this last time. He went with Chipper. They couldn't report it without admitting he was alive. I wondered if there were other lies the Olivers had told.

Everything seemed to connect and make sense, but I couldn't be sure. Maybe if I told someone else who wasn't as close to things as I was they'd tell me I was crazy.

I left the library and drove to Beth's house. Her Escort was in the driveway. When she answered the door her jeans and sweatshirt were covered with red paint.

"You wanna listen to a story?" I said.

"Sure." She motioned me inside. Then she wiped her hands on her jeans.

We sat on the couch in her living room. I stared at her glass coffee table. Its legs looked like tree branches.

"It's new," she said. "I'm just trying it out to see if I like it. What do you think?"

"If you run out of firewood, you can always use the legs."

"I should know better than to ask a man who thinks a LA-Z-BOY recliner is the height of contemporary furniture. Coffee?"

"Sure."

When she brought it I told her what I had been up to. I talked about Petey's latest disappearance, my conversation with Nash that got me thinking about the Olivers, the discs left on the table and how what I found at the Library made me think Chipper was alive.

She sat quietly until I was finished. Then she said. "I don't see it."

"Chipper wants me to find him. That's why he left the discs out on my table."

"Maybe it wasn't Chipper. Maybe it's someone trying to tell you something about him."

"Susan called him by name in the video."

Beth shrugged. "I don't know. It just seems unlikely a sixteen year old could fake his own death and hide out all this time."

"I know. Someone must have helped him. It had to be him I saw at the cemetery."

She shook her head. "You didn't get a real good look at him. I think you're letting your imagination run wild."

I took a sip of coffee and put the mug on the table. "You wanna take a ride to Hadley?"

She put a coaster under my mug. "You don't need me to go with you."

"I do. The guy I want to talk to wasn't too impressed with me. He might be more responsive to a beautiful woman."

She pushed her hair back from her forehead. "I meant what I said the other day." She took a sip of coffee and stared at one of her paintings on the wall. She turned back to me and her eyes narrowed. "Why don't you tell me what this is really about?"

"Okay. I think it would be good if we spent the day together, but besides that, there's a guy in Hadley that knows where Chipper is and you're going to get it out of him."

"Why would he tell me?"

"I don't know, but he sure as hell isn't going to tell me."

"Shouldn't the cops be doing this?"

"Chipper's been hiding from the cops for five years, but I'm convinced he wants me to find him. I want to know why."

She got up and brought her mug into the kitchen. I heard the faucet running and the door of the dishwasher open and close. She came back, sat down and sighed. "Why is it I always let you talk me into things?"

"Because you find me irresistible."

"No, that's not it." She shrugged. "I haven't been out to the

Connecticut River Valley in years. You buying dinner?"

Thirty minutes later we were cruising down Route 2. Vivaldi was on the tape deck, a concession to Beth's taste in music.

When we exited at Route 202, Beth said, "You sure they've stopped looking for Susan's killer?"

"Rita's usually pretty reliable and I had the feeling Nash was acting on his own when I talked to him."

As we passed through Amherst and into Hadley Beth was quiet. Then she said. "I'm glad you asked me to come."

It was close to one when I turned onto the road by the river. I drove past the cottages, stopped at the end of the Oliver driveway and stared at the cottage. The driveway was empty.

"Did you expect him to be here waiting for us?"

I shook my head. "I think he just uses it for private parties, but my guess is he doesn't live too far away."

"So why are we here?"

I pointed to the green Volkswagon van parked in the driveway across the field. "That's where the guy lives."

"I'm not sure about this, Steve. How am I supposed to get him to tell me about Chipper?"

"Improvise. You're good at that."

I reached in the back seat, grabbed my Red Sox cap and pulled the brim down so it touched my sunglasses.

"You look silly in a hat," Beth said.

"Maybe I should wear a pair of those funny glasses with the big nose and mustache."

I drove down his driveway and parked beside his van. The man must have heard the car because he walked out onto his porch. He had on the same denim shirt, chinos and work boots he wore the last time I saw him. His eyes narrowed and his ponytail swished as he walked slowly down his steps.

Beth took a long breath.

"You need me I'm just a few feet away," I said.

She jumped out of the car, and moved quickly in his direction. I rolled down my window so I could hear better. "We're looking for Chipper's place," she said. "Big party tonight and we're lost. I told him to turn left. Can you help me out?"

The man shielded his eyes from the sun and looked toward the car. "Where you coming from?"

"Just moved into Northampton. Chipper invited us to the party. Names Demi. You gonna be at the party?"

The man smiled. "I'm Jerry. No. I'm not going, but maybe you could pay me a visit later. Bring me some beer or something."

"I'd like that," Beth said.

Jerry smiled. He pushed his ponytail behind his collar and pulled in his gut. "Oliver place is right across the field." He pointed. "No one calls it Chipper's place anymore cause he's dead. Died about five years ago."

Beth looked toward the car and frowned. "That's kinda strange. Guy who invited us said his name was Chipper."

Jerry shrugged. "Someone's playing a joke on you."

"Shit," she said. "I wonder if there really is a party. Any idea how I can get ahold of the owner?"

"Truth is I don't know anything about who uses the cabin." He squinted toward the car. "Who's your friend?"

"He's my dentist." She leaned close to him and whispered in his ear.

Jerry laughed and whispered something back. Then he put his hand on her shoulder. She pulled away.

"Shit." I jumped out of the car and moved quickly. When I got a few inches away I pointed my finger. "Hands off, Jerry."

His eyes widened and I knew he recognized me.

"You were here a few days ago," he said. "What're you trying to pull?"

"Chipper's kidnapped his brother. The police are on their way to get him. We want to warn him. We could use your help finding him."

"I don't know what kind of bullshit you're up to, but you better get out of here before I shoot you for trespassing."

I looked toward the river. A dock extended out into the water in front of his cabin. "You got a boat?" When he didn't respond, I said, "You heard Chipper's screams that night, didn't you? You went out to try and save him. He's not dead, but like you said to me the last time I was here, 'live and let live'. You knew what kind of man Chipper's father was. You wanted him to get away from that."

"Get the fuck out of here."

We got into the car and I slowly drove up the driveway. In my mirror I could see Jerry standing on his steps. Maybe I was wrong. Maybe Chipper was dead. Maybe I wanted him to be alive so much I couldn't see the truth.

"Sorry," I said.

"For What?"

"Putting you through that."

"You kidding? I loved it. Reminded me of the days I wanted to be an actress. You should have stayed in the car. I was gonna kick the guy in the balls."

I smiled. "Your dentist?"

"He didn't know anything," she said.

"Chipper's been hiding out for five years. I guess Jerry's not about to say he's alive to a stranger. Maybe you should've taken your clothes off, Demi."

"You'd have liked that."

"I could have snapped some pictures, got you on the cover of Vanity Fair."

I took a left at the end of the driveway, drove up a few hundred feet and stopped. I stared back toward Jerry's cabin.

"Why are you stopping?" Beth said.

"I think Jerry knows how to get ahold of Chipper. We're just going to wait for awhile. What'd you whisper in his ear after you told him I was your dentist?"

"I told him you were gay and meeting your boyfriend at the party. He said he could tell that by just looking at you."

We put on some classical music and sat there. The van never left the yard. Chipper never came to talk to us, either.

After about an hour, Beth said, "I'm starving."

"Me too. Why don't we take a ride to Northampton and eat some lunch. Then we can come back here."

"It'll be dark by then."

I shrugged. "So maybe this wasn't such a great idea."

"Sure it was. I got to listen to Vivaldi and Bach. Now I'm getting a free lunch."

Salty's Tavern was just outside of Northampton Center, downstairs from a fancy restaurant. It had a long bar on the left and booths and tables on the right. A dartboard was on the back wall. It smelled of stale tobacco and spilled beer. At three in the afternoon there were only a few people seated at the bar.

We ordered drinks and burgers. After the waiter brought my Coke and Beth's white wine, I said, "Did you know I had a crimson aura?"

"I always suspected."

"It's probably what attracted you to me."

She stared at me. "No, but I do like the gray hairs. Maybe it means you're growing up."

"So you're reconsidering what you said the other day about dumping me?"

She took a sip of her wine. Her expression turned serious. "I didn't dump you. I just don't think we work as a couple."

"You're probably right. You need the serious type. The kind who would sit around the fire and read T.S. Eliot to you."

"Don't mock me."

The waiter picked that moment to bring our burgers. After he left I said, "Sorry."

Beth nodded and took a bite of her burger. We talked about a new exhibit opening at the Decordova and a book Beth was reading about Mozart. We reminisced about the summer we spent in Majorca when we visited his house. Then I told her about the school committee meeting on Monday.

"Are you worried?"

"Sure. If they decide to suspend me and the investigation drags on I could be out for weeks. I'm not sure how I'll handle being away from the classroom for that long."

She nodded. "I know how much you love it. I'll go to the meeting with you if you'd like."

I nodded. "Lisa's going to represent me."

We finished our burgers, had coffee and the waiter brought our check. I gave him my credit card.

Beth put her hand over her eyes. "You don't still have that picture on your card?"

A couple of years ago I had glued a picture of Richard to my Visa. The waiter looked at the card, then at me.

"It was taken when I had a beard," I said. "That's why it doesn't look like me."

He shook his head and left.

"What should we do now?" Beth said.

"First, I'm gonna take my crimson aura to the men's room. We can figure out what to do when I get back."

The men's room was downstairs and at the end of a long hall. It had one of those silhouette pictures on the door that made it hard to tell if it was the men's or ladies room, especially if you'd had a few drinks. I picked what I hoped was the men's room, pushed the door open a few inches, saw the urinal and went inside.

I splashed water on my face and stared at my gray hairs in the mirror. I was about to use the urinal when Chipper Oliver walked into the room.

CHAPTER 23

He was a tall man with a round face and a small thin-lipped mouth. He wore a Yankees cap and a fleece-lined denim jacket. His hair flipped out from under his hat and covered his ears. He looked like an older version of Petey. He leaned his back against the door and smiled.

I smiled back. "I was beginning to think I might be wrong."

"I do like those oldies," he said.

"You wanna tell me why you put McKinley's clothes in my closet?"

"In due time, Mr. Teacher."

Someone pushed on the door. It opened a few inches. Chipper leaned against it hard and said, "Use the other one. We're busy." Then he turned to me. "Give me ten dollars."

"You tailed me here to ask for money?"

"Typical teacher. Always asking questions." He held out his hand.

We played the kids game of who would blink first. Then he smiled and said, "Okay. Make it five."

I took out my wallet and handed him a bill. He examined both sides. "This is my retainer. I'm your lawyer."

"I'm not in the mood for games."

He handed the money back to me. "And you're my lawyer. Everything we're gonna talk about is confidential. That's something I value in life."

"Is Petey with you?"

"Petey's my concern. Now why don't you go tell your pretty woman you're going for a walk with a friend. I'll meet you outside."

Chipper looked in the mirror, pushed his hair back over his ears, then walked out the door.

I went back to the table. Beth was watching a hockey game.

"Chipper wants to talk to me. He's outside."

Her eyes widened. "No, shit. You want me to come? I'd kinda like to meet this guy."

I shook my head. "Do you mind waiting?"

I walked to the bar and ordered Beth another white wine then went outside.

Dusk had just settled in. Chipper was leaning against a giant oak smoking a miniature cigar.

I tugged up the zipper on my jacket and put my hands in my pocket. "The police think McKinley killed Susan," I said. "They're not pushing the investigation."

He took a puff on the cigar and started to walk down the sidewalk. "I love this town. I wouldn't want to live anyplace else. Course, I don't live here."

I put my hand on his shoulder and he stopped. "I didn't come out here to listen to your bullshit. I want to be sure Petey's all right and I thought you might know why Susan made the video. Maybe we can figure out who might have killed her."

"You disappoint me, teach. Don't you have any questions like how I faked my own death and why I let you find me?"

"Okay," I said. "Whatever you want to tell me, but is Petey all right?"

He took a puff of the cigar and watched the smoke curl into the air. "Petey's fine. He says you can be trusted. That's why you're gonna help me find Susan's killer."

I tried to read his expression, but he turned away from me and looked toward the road. "The police have the best chance of that," I said. "They've got the authority, manpower and the skills. Let's talk. If we come up with something I'll take it to the cops."

A woman walked by us, her head tucked low against the cold. Chipper watched her, then turned to me.

"You never really knew Susan, man. She was a good woman. Sweet, decent, innocent. A beautiful human being. Being around her made you want to be better. Hell, she made you feel like you could. Someone destroyed all that. I find out who, I'll kill 'em." He took another puff on his cigar. "You have any idea how much it hurt not being with the family at Susan's funeral? It hurt like hell, but I couldn't take the chance."

"Why? No one's looking for you. It's not like you committed a crime."

He flipped up the collar of his jacket so it covered the bottom half of his face. "Know why you're gonna help me? Because it's been over a week since Susan was murdered. The cops have gone on to other things. They're not gonna keep looking for the killer of a poor white girl. Especially if you're right and they think McKinley did it."

"You sure he didn't?"

He ignored my question. "You're gonna have the value of my expertise. You can nose around in places I can't."

"The only way I'm going to help is by taking what you know and going to the cops."

He smiled. "I'm a student of human nature. You'll help me 'cause you care about us. You proved that by going after Petey yourself and not calling the cops."

"Did you know Susan was pregnant?"

"She told me. Wouldn't say who the father was, though."

"Tell me about the video."

"See," he said. "You're acting like a cop already. Okay. Susan was into some scary shit."

"What scary shit?"

"Not sure. Someone had something on her and made her do the video." He looked into the window of a leather shop. "She always told me things, but not this. She didn't want to do it. Figured she might be able to relax if I filmed it. Took awhile but I finally got it."

"You don't know much."

"I know enough."

"Susan had an affair with McKinley. Why couldn't it have been his kid?"

He laughed. "She never did him. She hated him. Called him the weasel. Funny thing was she did know a lot about him."

"This is a waste of time."

"Look. I'm being open with you. I took a chance just talking to you. I'll tell you one thing for certain. Damon Saulnier didn't blow up McKinley. Guy was an asshole, but he had trouble putting gas in his car never mind rigging up a fancy bomb. If he were involved someone helped him."

"Is that why you put McKinley's clothes in my closet? As a message to the cops."

He shook his head. "Cops are stupid. It was a message for you. Plus I wanted to see if you were smart enough to find me."

"Why not just contact me yourself."

"I thought about it. Hell, I drove by your house a few times trying to make up my mind."

"The blue Chevy."

He nodded. "Then when the cops arrested Damon I knew I had to do something. I planted a few clues and then left it up to fate. I'm a strong believer in fate. Things happen for a reason. Now you're here and we're gonna help each other."

"Susan told people we dated. She wrote things in her diary we never did. Any idea why?"

"She takes after me. Always lookin' over her shoulder. Not wanting people to be too close. She got a kick out of being outrageous. Messin' with people's minds. Who knows what she was thinking."

"Did Petey know you were alive?"

He shook his head. "We were gonna tell him when he got older, but he suspected. When he saw the video he figured it out and came lookin' for me."

I stopped walking and turned back toward the tavern. "I was hoping you might know more," I said. "There's no way I'm going to look for Susan's killer."

He nodded and we started to walk back. "Let me tell you a story. Then if you still don't want to help, well, I took my shot and lost."

"Okay."

"You met Molly, Susan's friend?"

"I talked to her. She didn't tell me much. Kept talking about my aura."

"That's Molly, all right. She's crazy. Always talking about psychic shit and hearing voices, but Susan liked her. Something happened between them. I think it was over a man. Things had been strained. Susan told me that Molly was scaring her lately, but she was gonna patch things up. If you're gonna go to a deserted pond at two in the morning you bring someone close. I think Molly killed Susan."

"Come on, I was hoping for better from you. You think it was Molly at the amusement park shooting at us? How about McKinley? She blow him up too?"

"That's exactly what I think and we can prove it."

"How?"

"That's where you come in. I want you to tail her. Stick to her like a piece of tape on the sole of a shoe. You do that and she'll crack. I know it."

"Nice theory, but I didn't hear any proof in it and I've no intention of tailing anyone. I appreciate your telling me Petey's all right."

We reached the front of the tavern. "I dropped him at the mall. He's watching some kung-fu movie. Hell, he'd watch it ten times if I let him. He's fine. We're getting reacquainted. I'm not gonna take him home until Susan's killer is caught. Now, let's go inside and talk to your lady."

Beth was just finishing her wine when we entered. I introduced her to Chipper. "Let me buy this round," he said.

I sat down across from Beth. Chipper went to the bar.

"Is Petey with him?" Beth said.

I nodded. "He thinks Molly killed Susan. He wants me to tail her, but I'm not going to."

"Good," she said.

Chipper brought a white wine and two Heinekens. He put one of the beers in front of me.

"How'd you know I drink Heineken?"

"Told you I was a student of human nature." He smiled. "Petey told me. What kind of a teacher are you, anyway, discussing beers with a thirteen year old?"

I shrugged. "He asked me what kind of beer I drank and I told him."

We moved to a table away from the bar. Chipper spent the next thirty minutes talking. He told us how Susan helped him escape from his abusive father, how he lived with a couple of her friends in Springfield until he was eighteen then went off on his own. "I stayed wherever I could and supported myself by doing whatever it took. I just kept moving. I was always afraid my old man would track me down." He grinned. "Should have known better. Guy was to busy hiding out so he wouldn't have to pay child support."

"Jerry knew you were alive."

Chipper nodded. "Susan and I flipped the boat so it'd look like an accident. Then I climbed into the boat she was in. Jerry saw her, but he never told. He knew what my old man was like."

We talked for awhile longer, then Chipper said, "Why don't you follow me to the mall. I bet Petey would like to say hello."

The mall was outside town. Chipper went into the theater while Beth and I sat in the car. After about fifteen minutes I began to worry.

"What's taking them so long," Beth said, then her eyes widened and she pointed across the parking lot. Chipper was racing toward us, waving his arms. I jumped out of the car.

"Fuck," he said. "Petey's not inside. God damn kid's missing."

CHAPTER 24

"Damn it," I said. "You never should have left him alone."

Chipper took off his cap and pushed his fingers through his hair. His gaze darted around the parking lot.

"You check in the mall?"

He didn't respond.

"What about security. Maybe they saw him?"

He took several short quick breaths. "Theatre owner said someone called asking for Petey. Said it was an emergency. Owner didn't want to get him, but the woman told him exactly where Petey was sitting. Right where I put him in the last row. Son of a bitch must have tailed us. Petey talked to her, then left. That was over an hour ago."

"Did the owner see who he went with. Maybe he got into a car."

"Guy didn't see anything."

Beth moved beside me. "We've gotta call the cops."

"Bullshit. They couldn't find Petey the last time. I'll handle this. I got my underground. More connections than the cops. We'll find out who did this and I'll kill the bastard. You go back to Waltham. Follow Molly. If she didn't do this, she knows who did."

"I'll call Nash," I said. "He'll check out Molly."

Chipper pointed his finger at me and I saw anger in his eyes. "Don't fuck with me, man." He put his hands in the air. "Look. Give me till midnight tomorrow. I don't find Petey we'll do it your way."

I shook my head. "It may be too late. The cops can talk to people here. Maybe someone saw something."

"My men will do that. The cops will just get in my way."

"Chipper, whoever took Petey could've killed Susan."

"You don't think I know that."

"Petey tell you anything about the murder?" Something that may help us figure out who he went with."

"Told me he knew something. Wouldn't tell me what. I figured I had time to get it out of him." He shook his head. "Petey's not gonna go off with someone he doesn't know. Kid's too smart for that."

I looked at Beth, then refocused on Chipper. "I'll do what you ask on one condition. You find out who did it, you go to the cops. Don't do anything yourself."

"Deal." He sprinted toward his car.

"I think you've just been had," Beth said.

We watched as Chipper drove out of the lot.

"Did you notice how he wasn't in any hurry," I said. "If it were my brother I'd want the National Guard here. I think he knows where Petey is. I'll give him until tomorrow. I didn't say I wouldn't mention other things to the cops, just that I wouldn't report Petey's disappearance."

"Do you really trust him?"

"I think he cares about Petey's safety."

"I still think it's a mistake," Beth said.

"I hope not."

I dropped Beth at her place, waited until I saw the lights go on in her living room, then drove away.

Richard cooed as I walked in the door. There were two messages on my machine. One was from Aaron Fleming and the other from Jim Boyer, the director of Waltham's homeless shelter. I had started doing volunteer work there when I separated from Beth. A couple of times a month at first, but during the past year I had been there twice a week. I called the shelter.

"We've missed you," Jim said.

"Believe me, I miss being there. It's been tough lately."

We talked for awhile about Susan and Petey. I didn't mention his latest disappearance. Then Jim said, "Can we count on you to help us serve dinner again this Thanksgiving?"

"I can help set up in the morning, but I'm cooking a turkey this year. My mother, Dave and Mildred are coming over."

"Maybe they could help. You could eat late."

"They might like that. Let me check. I'll get back to you."

I cut up some French bread, added garlic butter and popped it in the microwave. Then I opened a bottle of Chianti, poured a glass and started to watch a John Wayne movie on television. John was tracking down an Indian played by Sal Mineo who had kidnapped Natalie Wood. Somehow I knew he'd catch him and my mind started to wander. A couple of months ago when I decided to do Thanksgiving at my place, I had pictured Beth at the table, and I thought we'd all have a lot to be thankful for. Funny how things turn out. I wondered what the Olivers were doing for Thanksgiving.

I fell asleep on the couch and when I woke up the sun was shining in through the window. I put on coffee and read the Sunday Globe sports page for awhile. I couldn't focus. I kept waiting for the phone to ring. A local talk show was on television and I put the volume on low. It felt good to hear another voice in the house. The Patriots were playing the Dolphins this afternoon and the Globe made it sound like the showdown of the century. Somehow I couldn't get too excited.

When James Carberry's face appeared on the television screen I turned up the volume. He was talking about Frank Mitchell, McKinley's opponent in the election. Carberry had worked for Mitchell for awhile, then had joined McKinley when he decided to run. I thought about the last time I had seen Carberry. He had been making the announcement that McKinley had died.

"Ed would have wanted this," Carberry said. "He felt it was important to have a Republican Governor. Frank Mitchell represents everything good about the party. That's why I agreed to become Frank Mitchell's press secretary. All Republicans should unite behind Frank. It's what Ed McKinley would have wanted."

My mind flashed back to something Carberry had said to me on the phone once. "I'll do anything to insure my candidate wins."

I wondered if that included murder.

I listened for awhile longer, but couldn't concentrate. I kept going over things Carberry had said to me.

I picked up the phone and called Beth. "Anything on Petey?" she said.

"Nothing. Listen, you want company? I could pick up some food."

"I was planning on painting today."

"You gotta eat, right? I'll come over, make lunch and then you can go back to work." When she hesitated I said, "I got something I want to talk over with you."

"Steve, give me some space, okay."

"Sure."

"Let me guess. You wanted to talk to me about Susan's murder."

I told her about seeing Carberry on television and what I had been thinking. "Suppose he's been working for Mitchell all along and got Susan to make the video to destroy McKinley's campaign. Susan backs out, threatens to tell. Maybe asks for money so he kills her."

"You've been watching too many Oliver Stone movies."

"It could've happened."

"Don't you see what's happening to you. You're becoming obsessed. It's all you can talk about. Yesterday you thought Molly did it. Today it's Carberry. Who's it going to be tomorrow?"

"I'm sorry, but there's a lot at stake."

"Sure, it's important, but you're a teacher, not a cop. Let the police do their work."

"The cops aren't looking for Susan's killer."

"I find that really hard to believe. Steve, I've got some painting to do." She hung up.

I stared at the phone, then hung it up.

"Beautiful," I said aloud. "I'm trying to convince Beth to go out with me again and I get her so upset she hangs up on me."

I put my head back against the couch cushion. Maybe Beth was right. Maybe I was so obsessed with Susan's murder I wasn't thinking straight.

I called Lisa Gerrault and left a message on her machine explaining about Monday's meeting and asking her to call me. Then I called Aaron and we talked about Carberry for awhile. I could hear the excitement in his voice. He was going to do some checking on Carberry's connection to Mitchell.

I flipped on the Pats game and tried to watch, but I couldn't concentrate. I paced around the room. I had to do something.

Five minutes later I was parked in front of Rita Dooley's. Her car was in the yard and I rang the bell. When she opened the door her red hair was wet as if she had just taken a shower. "You want some company?" I said.

"Sure. I'm watching the Pats game."

I plopped down on her leather couch. Bright sun was streaming in through the window. The magazines which had been stacked on the coffee table the last time I visited were piled in a corner.

Rita got two beers out of the refrigerator and put them on coasters. Then she sat down, leaving about a foot of space between us. We watched the game, sipped on beers and talked about the Pats chances for making the playoffs.

"Are you okay?" Rita said.

"Fine."

She shook her head. "There's something wrong. I can tell."

"It's Susan's murder. I feel like I should be doing something to get the cops to find her killer."

"No. It's more than that. I can hear it in your voice. You're not sick or anything?"

I hesitated.

She touched my face. "You don't have to tell me, but if you need someone to talk to I'll listen. You know I'm always here for you."

"It's Beth. I want our relationship to work, but we're falling into the same patterns we had when we were married."

"Maybe she's not the right woman for you. If she makes you unhappy you should stop seeing her."

"That's just it. Most of the time she makes me happy."

She took a sip of her beer. "Did you talk to her? Tell her what's bothering you."

"That's the other thing. She wants me to tell her everything I'm thinking. That's not me."

"Seems to me you've got to make a decision. Your relationship will never get anywhere if you don't tell her what you need."

I nodded.

She watched the game for a few seconds. "Open up, for Chrissake. You can't keep hiding. You're using that as an excuse. You're afraid if you're honest with her it'll make you vulnerable and if she rejects you then it'll hurt worse. It's an instinct with you, but you gotta fight it if you want to patch things up."

I laughed. "I came over to make sure you're okay."

"It's easier to deal with someone else's problems sometimes. I've been keeping my mind occupied by doing some digging."

"Anything you can talk about?"

"What do you know about Cynthia Oliver?"

"Not much. She's lived in New York City for five years. Claims to be an actress."

"A cop I know in New York did some checking. She hasn't had an acting job in over a year. Fact is, she hasn't worked much at all. She lives alone in an apartment in the city. It's not much, but city rents can be high. Pays her rent every month and her car's only two years old. So where does she get her money?"

"Boyfriend?"

No one special in her life. She sure doesn't get the money from her family."

"Does she have a record?"

"Nothing."

"Did you ask her about it?"

"It's not my case. I mentioned it to Nash, but he didn't seem very interested."

"What the hell is going on?"

"I don't know, but I'm going to keep looking until someone tells me to stop."

I told her about seeing Carberry on television and my theory. Then I said, "Molly Franklin was her best friend, but they had a falling out. Maybe you could check on her, too."

"I'll see what I can find out about both of them, but it's not going to be easy."

We watched the game for awhile longer. It felt good to talk about Susan to someone who would listen. At half time I got up to leave.

"Thanks for the company," she said. "You wanna talk, I'm always here to listen."

I went home to check my messages. None. I sat for awhile wondering if Chipper would call. Maybe I was wrong. Maybe Chipper didn't know where Petey was, but was afraid to call in the cops. Maybe Beth was right and I'd been had. Then I thought about Molly. Chipper seemed convinced she'd killed Susan and knew something about Petey's disappearance. Why was he so certain I'd turn up something if I tailed her? I dialed her number. When she answered the phone I hung up.

Ten minutes later I was parked on her street, a few hundred feet from her brown two-story house. I put on a Little Richard tape and ran through all the reasons I was wasting my time, but the truth was, I felt exhilarated.

I wondered if Molly's father might look out the window and recognize my T-Bird. It looked out of place in this neighborhood and I knew I wouldn't be able to park long before someone got suspicious and called the cops. Twenty minutes if I was lucky.

Richard was belting out "Long Tall Sally" when a woman in the house next to Molly's looked out her window. I pretended to be playing with my radio, but when I looked up she was still there. I started the car, drove by Molly's house and waited on the other side. A couple of boys were in the street throwing a football. They kept looking toward my car.

Ten minutes later her front door opened. She hurried down the front steps and climbed into a red Firebird that sat in front of the house. Its engine roared. She made a U-turn and headed out toward Main Street. I gave her a little lead-time, then started the T-Bird and followed.

She cruised through the city. At first I thought she was going to the Chateau, where we had talked earlier, but she drove past it and on to Route 128 heading north.

Once we hit the highway I dropped back. Traffic was heavy and the farther she went the more I asked myself what the hell I was doing. When she exited at Route One through Topsfield, I was two cars behind her. About five miles later she flicked on her directional and turned into a motel called Cozy Acres. I looked at my clock. It was after five.

I drove by. Several units of the motel lined the street, but more were around the side and built diagonally toward the woods in back. The place looked like it had been built in the fifties and the owners hadn't bothered maintaining it.

I made a U-turn and pulled into the parking lot of a laundromat across the street just as she walked into the motel office. She was inside for a few minutes, then got back into her car and drove around the side of the motel.

I pulled back out onto Route One and drove by again. Molly had parked in front of the unit closest to the woods. Chipper's words echoed in my mind. "They had been fighting," he had said. "Probably over a man." My gut told me this wasn't a waste of my time. I wanted to know who she was meeting.

A drug store was about a quarter of a mile up the highway. I parked in the lot, got out of my car and made my way toward the motel. I cut through a field, walked into the woods behind the motel and hid behind a tree. I had a clear view of Molly's unit.

Forty-five minutes went by. The sky had clouded over, its stars hidden, the moon just a vague glimmer above the horizon. It had gotten colder. I zipped up my jacket and put my hands in my pockets. If it started to snow, it'd stick. A few minutes later lights flicked on outside of each unit.

I heard a voice in my mind, analyzing the situation, saying I was doing something pointless and foolish. I decided to wait a few more minutes. If nothing happened by then I'd leave.

A beige Tempo rounded the corner of the units and parked next to Molly's Firebird. The person in the car sat for a few seconds. The door to the unit opened and she got out of the car. Although I only had a view for a few seconds I recognized the spiked blond hair. It was Lois McKinley.

CHAPTER 25

I leaned against the tree and stared at the door. Chipper had said Molly and Susan had been fighting. He assumed it was over a man. What if it had been over Lois McKinley? I thought about all the reasons I should just go home, but I couldn't. I had to confront them.

I walked out of the woods toward the unit. The curtains were pulled tight. There were no other cars in the lot. I put my ear against the door. I could hear them talking softly, but couldn't make out what they were saying.

I pounded on the door. The talking stopped, but no one answered. I pounded again.

I heard footsteps and I knew someone was on the other side looking through the peephole. Then the door opened.

Molly's face turned red. "What the hell are you doing? You want me to call the cops?"

I looked behind her, but didn't see anyone. "Sure. I bet they'd be interested in what you're doing with Lois McKinley."

She looked back into the room and sighed. "What is it you want?"

"Some honest answers."

The door opened wider and Lois McKinley moved beside Molly. She wore a beige wrap-around skirt and a white silk blouse. Two gold chains hung around her neck.

"Did your husband know you were sleeping with Molly?"

She sighed. "Why don't you come in, Mr. Asher?"

Molly's eyes widened. "You don't have to say anything to him."

Lois touched her arm gently. "No, I don't, but maybe it'll help. I've done nothing to be ashamed of." She motioned me inside.

I looked in at the room and shook my head. "I'd be more comfortable out here."

Lois grabbed a jacket and we walked slowly toward the woods. The door slammed behind us.

"I should probably just ask you to leave, but I don't want you going around telling people things that aren't true. Who did you follow?"

"Molly. I thought she might know more about Susan's death than she's telling."

"She doesn't." She walked a few steps ahead of me. "It's not what it looks like. Molly was helping me sort out my feelings."

"In a motel room?"

She broke a twig off a branch and stopped walking. "I've been getting a lot of publicity lately. We'd have more privacy here." She threw the twig on the ground. "I loved Susan. I'm trying to come to grips with my loss."

I studied her. "Did your husband know?"

She looked up at the sky and pulled the collar of her jacket up. "I told him. We hadn't been getting along for awhile, but a divorce would be bad for the campaign. I met Susan at one of Ed's functions. She was so intelligent and caring. It just happened. Funny thing was, Ed said he had an affair with her to protect me."

"He must have loved you very much."

She looked at me with a quizzical expression. Then she turned and slowly headed back toward the motel. I followed her.

"Do you know who got Susan pregnant?"

She shook her head. "Susan was secretive. I respected her enough not to push her. If she wanted me to know, she'd tell me."

I put my hand on her shoulder and she stopped. "Why are you telling me all this?"

"I'm going to tell everyone about my relationship with Susan. It's what Molly and I are discussing. She thinks I shouldn't. What do you think?"

"It's your decision, but, yeah, I think you should be honest."

We walked in silence. When we reached the unit, she said, "I want to tell people on my time-table and my own terms. I hope you'll respect that."

"Of course."

She narrowed her eyes. "You look like you have something else on your mind."

"I was wondering if you're surprised Carberry is working for Frank Mitchell."

"Nothing James Carberry does surprises me. He is a man without principal, but if you're asking me do I think he killed Ed, I don't. He respected Ed too much for that." She hesitated. "One word of advice, Mr. Asher. Stop playing the sleuth. It could get you into trouble."

"The police have stopped looking for Susan's killer."

"It was my understanding they had reached a dead end."

"That's funny. A cop told me it was your family that was putting pressure on them."

She shrugged. "Parents will go to any extreme to protect their children. Do you have kids, Mr. Asher?"

"No."

"A shame. My three children have been very supportive." She held out her hand and we shook. "You're a decent man. You'd make a good father." She opened the door and walked inside.

A light snow started to fall as I headed back to Waltham. Lois McKinley had been open with me, almost too open. I wondered how truthful she had been. Her words echoed in my mind. "Parents will go to any extreme to protect their children."

With the shock of seeing Lois and Molly I had forgotten to ask if Molly knew about Petey. Thing was, it didn't bother me. I was beginning to think Molly didn't have anything to do with Susan's murder or Petey's disappearance. As I crossed the city line my gut was telling me that the reason for Susan's murder rested with the Olivers.

It was close to ten when I pulled in front of their house. The lights were on in the living room and the curtains were drawn. I wasn't sure what I was going to say. I just knew I wanted to talk. Confront them. Tell them I knew about Chipper. See what they'd say. I was tired of their secrets and I wanted things out in the open. I rang the bell.

Mrs. Oliver opened the door. She had on a gray housecoat and when she recognized me she pulled it tight around her neck. She smiled, but didn't make a move to let me in.

"I know Chipper's alive," I said, "What I don't know is why you want to keep it a secret."

She closed the door. When she opened it a few seconds later she had a coat on. She moved out on the porch and shut the door. "Cynthia's asleep. She wouldn't like it if she knew I was talking to you."

"Why? What's she afraid of?"

She looked at the snow falling lightly from the sky. "Nothing. You have to understand Cynthia. She's always had this dream of being an actress. It's not coming true. Maybe she doesn't have the talent. I don't know, but trying to come to grips with Susan's murder has made her angry." She hesitated. "Now what's this about Chipper?"

I explained how I tracked him down in Northampton.

"I've nothing to say to you. Will you please leave?"

"Look," I said, "tomorrow night the school committee may suspend me because they think I had something to do with Susan's death. The cops aren't investigating, so it's up to me. I'll do anything to find the killer. What I need from you is the truth or I'm going to the cops."

"What do you mean the cops aren't investigating? Why not?"

"I don't know. Maybe there's not enough evidence. Maybe someone's put pressure on them. I just know they've stopped."

She gripped the railing so tight her knuckles turned red.

"Petey's not with Chipper," I said.

"'Course he is."

I shook my head. "Chipper lost him. He went off with someone. Mrs. Oliver, we both want the same thing don't we?"

She rubbed her eyes with her hand and her shoulders sagged. "It's been so long since I talked to anyone about Chipper. You must promise me you won't go to the police."

"If I feel he has something to do with Susan's murder I have to."

"No. No. Chipper would never... He's a good boy. He's got a legitimate job and a new identity. He doesn't want his old life back."

"You're not telling me the truth. He was too scared to come to Susan's funeral. Why?"

She turned away from me. When she turned back she was frowning. "Sometimes he loses his temper."

"Did he lose it with Susan. Is that what you're trying to tell me."

"No. He loved Susan. He wanted to protect her. He just gets these thoughts that if someone does the family wrong they have to pay. He used to frighten me, but that was years ago. Now he's got it under control."

She reached for the door handle. I couldn't let her go inside. There was something she wasn't telling me. I had to find out.

"Damon Saulnier told me your family kept secrets. What else are you hiding?"

For a brief moment the color drained from her face. "Saulnier's a psychopath. He killed McKinley. When I heard Susan was dead he was the first person I thought of." She opened the door and started to go in. Then she turned. "You don't know what you're doing." She went inside and closed the door.

The snow had stopped, but a thin coating covered my windshield. I pushed it off with my hand, then sat inside for awhile, staring at the house. I banged my hand on the steering wheel. She was so close to telling me something about Chipper. I felt she wanted to, but something was holding her back. If he didn't kill Susan what did he do that the family is covering up. I put my head back and closed my eyes. I felt tired, emotionally drained. Maybe a good nights sleep would clear my head and make things clearer.

The message light on my machine was flickering when I walked into my apartment. I pushed the button. "Asher. You call me right away. I got to talk to you." He left a number. I could hear the anger in Chipper's voice. I punched out his number.

"You leave my family alone," he said.

"Did you find Petey, because if you didn't I'm calling the cops and I'll tell them you're still alive.

"I told you I'd find him."

"Put him on."

"He's asleep."

"Bullshit. I need the truth. It's the only way we may be able to find Susan's killer."

"I told you the truth."

"Why are you paying Cynthia's rent?"

I could hear him breathing heavily. Then he said, "Why I pay her rent is none of your business. Look I confided in you because Petey said you could be trusted. I thought we could work together, but

I'm beginning to feel different and it makes me angry. You don't want to see me angry."

"Did you know Susan was having an affair with Lois McKinley?"

"Who?"

"Edward McKinley's wife."

"Why would you say that?"

I told him about tailing Molly and what I saw. I thought if he knew he might be honest with me.

"That bitch," he said. "It's starting to make sense to me."

"You want to tell me what you're talking about?"

There was silence on the other end of the phone. Then he said, "I knew I was right. It's all coming together. Susan said some things to me I didn't tell you. How could I have been so stupid." He hesitated. "I'm coming to Waltham. I'm gonna take care of Molly Franklin." His voice was low, but the words went right through me.

"Hang on," I said. "We don't really know anything. This isn't the time to act impulsively. Let me do some more checking and see what I can find out."

"Bullshit. You did your job." His voice rose. It sounded shaky, like he had lost control. "Now I'm gonna do mine. Petey's with me. Always been with me. I used you, Mr. Teacher. I knew if you thought he was in danger you'd tail Molly. All I needed was some proof" He hung up.

I sat on the couch and stared at the phone before hanging up. What the hell had I done? Everything seemed so logical. First, finding Chipper, then tailing Molly and telling him so he'd talk about his family, but on the phone he didn't seem rational. What had Susan told him about Molly? The longer I sat the more convinced I was he would kill her.

I dialed the Waltham Police. The officer on duty listened to my story. A cruiser would be sent to Molly's house, he said, but from his voice I could tell he didn't think it was urgent.

I had to warn her. I picked up the phone, then put it down. What if she didn't believe me? I'd have to convince her.

Ten minutes later I was ringing her doorbell and rehearsing what I was going to say if her father answered. Molly opened the door. "Jesus. What now Asher."

"You've got to leave the house."

She walked out on the porch and pulled the door closed. "What are you talking about?"

"Chipper thinks you killed Susan and he's on his way to get you."

"Chipper's dead," she said quietly.

"No he's not. He's living in Northampton, but I think you know that. I just talked to him."

"Susan told you?"

"No. I figured it out, but that doesn't matter. Just get out of the house. Go away for awhile. I called the cops. They'll pick him up. Then you can go home."

"Why would he think I killed Susan?"

"He knows about Lois McKinley."

"Jesus. You've got to reach him. It was Susan who seduced her. It was a game at first. Then she realized she cared for Lois. I tried to stop her. We fought and I said some stupid things I didn't mean. You got to tell him that. Chipper's crazy. No telling what he might do."

"Did Susan have an affair with Edward McKinley?"

"No. Someone forced her to make the video. I don't know who."

I wanted to ask her more, but I didn't have time. "Get out of the house," I said.

"All right. I'll let you know where I am. You can call me when it's safe."

"No. I'd rather not know. When it's safe I'll call your father."

She closed the door and went inside.

I went back home, double checked all the locks, then sat on the couch. An icy wind rattled the windows in their frames and the walls creaked. I thought about Edward McKinley. He was willing to give up everything to protect his wife's name. So who would want him dead?

It was after eleven-thirty when I dialed Rita's number. "I think I made a terrible mistake." I told her about finding Chipper and my conversations with Molly. I expected her to be upset. Instead she was quiet. "Rita," I said.

"Just thinking. They're definitely getting some cops to Molly's?"

"I think so."

"I'll double check. What's Chipper look like?"

I described him. Then I said, "Maybe I'm exaggerating. Maybe

Chipper's not going after Molly."

"Chipper's dangerous," she said.

I waited for her to say more. When she didn't I said, "What makes you say that?"

"I did some checking when you left this afternoon. The last place old man Oliver was seen was a small town in Vermont. I called the sheriff. He remembered him all right. Said Oliver disappeared one day and he'd always suspected someone killed him. Said a stranger had been seen in town around that time. He checked his records. Sounded like the description you just gave me of Chipper."

CHAPTER 26

She hesitated. "It was about three years ago. He left most of his clothes and some cash in the cabin he was living in. He'd just won a bet on a football game and never came to collect. There was no sign of foul play and the only thing unusual was the stranger the sheriff saw."

"Maybe the old man spotted Chipper and took off."

"Sheriff doesn't think so. About six months later a body was found in another county by a fisherman. It had been in the water for some time. Guy had been shot in the back of the head. The sheriff went to see the body, but it was so decomposed he couldn't tell if it was Oliver or not. Only way to check would have been through dental records, but Oliver didn't have any so it was dropped. Sheriff always suspected it was him though."

I felt a gnawing begin in the pit of my stomach as I remembered Chipper's words on the phone. "Mrs. Oliver told me he has a temper and would make anyone who harmed the family pay. The old man had abused Chipper and Susan. Then he didn't pay child support, but, Jesus, shooting his father in the head."

"You got a gun?"

"You kidding. Don't like them. Why?"

"If Chipper sees the cops at Molly's, he might think you betrayed him. He could come after you. We'll put a cruiser on your street. At least for tonight."

I rubbed my eyes with my fingers. "Thanks."

"Stay close to the phone. If we get him I'll call you."

I double-checked the locks and poured a scotch. Then I shut off all the lights except the one over the stove and sat on the couch. Richard cooed softly. The ice cubes tinkled against the side of the glass when I took a drink.

I listened for cars on the street, but at midnight everything was quiet. If a cruiser was out there I couldn't see it. Only the sound of the wind blowing through the trees disturbed the silence.

I took a sip and tried to picture where Chipper might be. If he left right away it would be at least another hour before he got to Molly's, assuming he went straight there. I banged my fist on the couch.

Thing was, I could feel his rage. He and his sister had been abused and then Susan was killed. I could understand his frustration and his need to do something about it. But why Molly? What had Susan told him?

I sat for awhile, feeling wired. I must have dozed because when the phone rang at six it woke me. It was Lisa Gerrault. She'd been away all weekend and just gotten my message. We talked about the committee meeting for awhile. It was scheduled for nine o'clock tonight and we made arrangements to meet in her office at seven. The meeting didn't seem so important to me now.

I called the police station, but the cop on duty wouldn't tell me anything. I showered, shaved and dressed. If the police had picked up Chipper, Rita would have called.

I looked up and down the street as I went to my car. If a cruiser had been on the street, it wasn't there now. I checked my mirror as I drove. No one seemed to be following. I wanted to stop at the Sacred Heart and say a few prayers, but I didn't want to be there by myself. Thing was, if Chipper was coming after me I'd put my kids at school in danger. I wouldn't take that chance. When I arrived I headed toward Mr. Webster's office.

He was talking on the phone when I tapped on his door. He motioned me to sit down.

When he finished I said, "I have to take today off."

He shook his head. "This is what I've been talking about. We can't have you taking off everytime you feel it's necessary."

"I'll get my lesson plans ready."

He glared at me. "I wanted to talk to you, anyway. The committee's going to suspend you tonight. They've got the votes. I just thought you should know."

I nodded. The meeting was the last thing on my mind.

"Why don't you get a couple of weeks worth of plans ready.

Hopefully, you'll be back before then."

I went to my room. There were teachers in the hallway. It made me feel safer. I opened the door to the next classroom, then sat in my chair. I looked at the books and the picture of Beth on my desk. I put together some plans, then got up and walked down the rows of wooden desks to the back of the room. I picked up a piece of yellow chalk and wrote the date on the blackboard. I rubbed some chalk dust between my fingers and put some on the tip of my tongue.

When the bell rang I was sitting at my desk. I heard the low murmur of the students get louder as they approached. Some giggled, some shouted, others greeted their friends as if they hadn't seen them in a long time. Lockers slammed and several students went by. I walked out of my classroom and closed the door.

"Morning, Mr. A.," Billy said. "You see the Pats game yesterday?"

I shook my head.

I left the building and drove to the library. I wanted to be in a place where there were people. I sat at a cubicle hidden from view. It gave me time to think.

Someone must have found out that Chipper was still alive and killed his father. They forced Susan to make the video. I couldn't imagine a member of her own family killing her, not even Chipper with his temper. When Susan met Lois McKinley she must have changed her mind. I thought about James Carberry. He could have killed Susan to keep her quiet. Maybe McKinley found out and Carberry killed him too. But what was Petey's medallion doing at the murder scene and why did Susan write about me in her diary?

At ten-thirty, I went to a pay phone. First, I called the police station, but couldn't find out anything. I left a message on Rita's machine telling her where I was. Then I called Aaron Fleming at the Trib.

"Where've you been?" he said. "I tried to reach you."

"Beth and I went out to Northampton on Saturday."

"You two getting serious? I think it's great."

"I may be the only one getting serious," I said. "Reason I called, have you heard anything about a police stake-out over on Brewster Street?"

He hesitated. "No. What's going on over there?"

"I'm not sure."

"Sure you are. I can tell by your tone. You wanna tell me what's really on your mind?"

"Look, I got this school committee meeting tonight. It looks like I'm going to have a lot of free time starting tomorrow. We'll talk. I want my side of the story printed and I've got some things that are bothering me about Susan's murder. I'd like you to check them out."

"You want to give me a hint?"

"Tomorrow. I need time to sort things out."

"Maybe I'll take a run over to Brewster. See what's going on."

"Not a good idea. The cops are looking for someone. You'll get in the way."

"Got anything to do with Susan's murder?"

"Aaron, I've already said too much. I'll talk to you tomorrow."

"You want some company tonight?"

"Beth's coming and I've got a lawyer. The meeting's in executive session, but thanks."

"Good luck," he said.

By four o'clock I was back in my apartment. I checked all of the rooms. Nothing. Then I double locked the doors. There was a message from Beth on my machine. "Call me as soon as you get in. It's important."

I dialed her number. After it rang several times I hung up. She must have forgotten to put her machine on. I hoped she wasn't canceling out on me tonight.

I put Eddie Cochran on the player and sat on the couch. Any time I heard a car on the street I went to the window. When I looked at the clock it was after five. I called Beth again. Still no answer. Her mother lived in New York and had been sick recently. Maybe something happened. But why wouldn't she leave the message on my machine? I felt sure she'd call before I left for the meeting.

I fed Richard, then got a couple of pieces of Italian bread and slapped peanut butter on it. While I ate I went over what I wanted to say to the committee.

It was after six when I put on my suit. I called Beth again. Still no answer. She had said it was important. So where the hell was she?

It was dark when I left my apartment. I drove by Beth's on my way to Lisa's. Her Escort was parked in the driveway. All the lights were off in the house except the one in the bathroom. I jumped out of the car, jogged up the front steps and rang the bell. When she didn't come I banged on the door, then tried to open it. It was locked.

I walked along the front of the house and tried to see inside, but the curtains were drawn lightly. I told myself that the uneasiness I was feeling was unjustified. She'd gone out with a friend. That's why her car was still in the yard. She'd probably still come to the meeting.

Around the back of the house three steps led into the kitchen. I tried the door. Locked. I leaned against the railing and looked toward the house next door. Then I picked up a rock. If Beth was okay we could laugh about the time I broke her window.

The breaking glass sounded like a loud explosion. I reached inside and unlocked the door. It swung open, all the way around on its hinges until it banged into the wall. "Beth," I yelled as I flipped on the light. No response. Two glasses stood on the plastic drainer, freshly rinsed. A container of Orange Juice was on the counter.

I moved quickly through the doorway between the kitchen and living room, turning on the overhead light and looking left and right as I crossed the threshold.

The couch cushions lay on the far side of the room as if someone had flung them there, but the rest of the room seemed untouched. Beside an armchair was Beth's pocketbook. She never went anywhere without it. My heart started to race.

I flipped on the hallway lights. Beth's bedroom was on the left, her studio on the right. Both doors were closed. I glanced into the bathroom as I went by, then pushed open the bedroom door. Her bed was made, the closet door open. Everything appeared normal.

A gusty breeze blew tree branches against the side of the house. Inside the silence seemed to grow deeper.

I opened the door to the studio. Nothing. A painting rested on her easel.

That left only the basement.

I opened the door and flicked on the lights below. The plank stairs creaked as I made my way down. Three minutes later I was back upstairs.

I was heading toward the kitchen to call the cops when I spotted her purse again. I picked it up to see if her wallet was inside. That's when I saw something glistening in the light in front of the TV and over by the wall. A dark red stain on the rug about the size of a quarter. It still looked wet. I bent down, touched the tip of my finger against the carpet and lifted it to my nostrils. It was blood.

CHAPTER 27

"Oh shit, oh shit, oh shit," I said.

I reached for the phone on the table. No dial tone. The wire had been ripped from the wall.

I walked quickly into the kitchen. That phone was still connected, but when I picked it up I saw a note that had been folded and taped to the receiver. The words were in large block letters. "If you call anyone she's dead. Go home. I'll contact you."

I slammed down the receiver so hard the plastic cracked. I couldn't call the cops. Not with Beth's life at stake.

When I entered my apartment I wondered how I got there. I didn't remember covering the in-between roads.

There were no messages on my machine. I sat on the couch with my hand on the phone willing it to ring. Ten minutes passed and I began to think they wouldn't contact me by phone. Maybe something had been left in the apartment.

I checked each room, then the stairway and front door. I was back on the couch staring at the phone when it rang.

The voice was high-pitched and squeaky, like it had been recorded on tape and was being played at a different speed. "Park in the church lot near Walden. If you don't do as I say I'll kill her. She'll be in front of the bath house. Do you understand?"

"I'll do anything you want," I said.

The phone disconnected.

I stood up, but my legs were weak and wobbly. Stay calm, I told myself. You can't help Beth if you lose control. There weren't any rules for this. I had to do what I felt was right, not just for Beth, but for me too. I couldn't live with myself if I called the cops and things went wrong. There was no one I could get to help. It was up to me. I tried to wipe the thought that she could already be dead out of my mind, but it stayed. I had to check. I dialed Rita Dooley.

"Steve, I meant to call you. We haven't seen any sign of Chipper. Maybe you read him wrong or maybe he realized there was a stake-out. Has he tried to contact you?"

"No." I hesitated. "Has anybody been hurt in town? Anyone taken to the hospital?"

"You mean Molly? No. We've no idea where she is."

"What about anyone else?"

"Anyone else? Are you all right, Steve?"

"Yeah. I guess everything is just getting to me. Sorry to bother you."

"You're not bothering me. You got the school committee meeting tonight. You want to talk about it."

"No," I said. "I'll take care of everything."

I took off my tie and sport coat, then slipped on my parka. I walked into the kitchen and opened the silverware drawer. I took out a knife. It had a wooden handle and a six or seven inch blade. I touched the tip, then slipped it into my coat pocket.

"Take care of yourself," I said to Richard.

As I drove my mind flashed back to Beth's. There had been no sign of forced entry. She had let the person in. It had to be some-body she knows.

The church lot was empty and dark. I opened my glove compart-ment, took out my flashlight and tested it. Then I flashed it toward the church. There were plenty of places for a person to hide. If not here, then up on the road. I slowly opened my car door and got out. I jogged up the hill and began to walk along the main road. The pond was about two miles away. A set of headlights approached and I moved into the trees beside the road and waited until they passed.

I moved quickly flashing my light in different directions. I don't remember if any other cars passed or what buildings I walked by. When I saw Walden from the road it looked quiet and peaceful.

The moon glistened off the water as I cut across the parking lot and down an embankment toward the bathhouse. When I reached the steps leading to the beach I stopped. All I heard was the wind. Then I walked down the stairs toward the water.

Beth wasn't in front of the building. I checked the sides, looking right and left. Nothing. I squinted and scanned the shoreline. The moon illuminated the beach and the trail that circled the pond.

I flashed the light into the woods and back-pedaled toward the water. I felt a tightening in my stomach. I stood still for a few minutes. Then I figured out where Beth had to be.

In the same place I found Susan.

I started to jog. I passed the boat landing, then raced along the winding path, jumping over stumps and rocks.

The wire fence was on my right and up ahead I saw it lying in the path exactly as it had been the night I found Susan. I stopped jogging and began to walk slowly. I pointed my light down toward the water.

She was sitting below me in the sand, facing the path. Even in the darkness she looked pale and drawn. Her hands were clutched together at her waist, her shoulders hunched. A rope was wound around her and thick black tape was wrapped around her mouth. Her eyes widened and her shoulders moved as she struggled to get up.

"Beth," I yelled and scampered down the slope.

I flashed my light on her face. A gash on her temple was oozing blood. Her jaw had turned a dark blue.

Then I heard the sound of footsteps clomping on the path behind me. I flashed my light toward the sound. Aaron Fleming stood about fifty feet away, his gun leveled at me. The sight sent a sudden surge of terror through my body.

He flashed his light in my eyes. "Untie her."

I took the tape from her mouth. "Honey, are you all right?"

She took several short quick breaths and nodded.

I loosened the knot, slipped the rope over her head and hugged her close to me.

"Move away from her," Fleming said.

I straightened, then reached into my pocket and felt the sharpness of the knife blade.

He must have noticed my movement. "Take your coat off."

"It's freezing."

"Take it off and throw it over here where I can see it." He motioned with his light.

I unbuttoned my coat, slipped it off my shoulders and tossed it a few feet away. It was then I realized what his plan was. Our deaths would look like a murder/suicide. I couldn't live without Beth so I killed her and then turned the gun on myself. I could see the headline he'd write and the lies he'd put in his story about the guilt I felt over Susan. It frightened me, but also made me angry.

I turned back to Beth. "We'll get out of this," I said loudly. "I called the cops. They'll be here any minute."

Aaron laughed. The light was focused on my face when I turned. "I know you, Steve. You wouldn't risk her life by doing something stupid. It's just the three of us."

I heard the click of the safety.

"Put the gun down," I said. "We're not going anywhere."

He laughed. "No, I suppose you're not, but that's the point isn't it?"

I shielded my eyes with my hand. "It won't work. The cops will see the rope marks."

"They'll just think you tied her up," he said. "It doesn't matter. Nothing will connect me to this."

I turned my back and moved closer to Beth so I stood between her and where Aaron was standing on the path.

"Move away from her," he said.

"If you shoot me in the back your plan won't work, will it? Why don't you come down and make me move away?"

His breathing got heavier and I heard the sound of his footsteps move along the path. Out of the corner of my eye I saw the beam of his flashlight move.

I looked up, noted his movement and inched to a new position staying between him and Beth.

"Maybe I'll change my plan," he said. "I'll write how upset Beth was about you and Susan. She kills you and then herself. Is that what you want?"

"I know why you killed Susan and it'll be just a matter of time before the cops figure it out."

"You don't know anything."

"You're a real ladies man, Aaron. I bet you really charmed Susan at first. You got her pregnant. Then told her she could make a lot of money if she accused McKinley. You made her follow him and try to seduce him. It didn't work."

"Shut up."

"You didn't care about the money, You just wanted to reveal the video and write that big story."

He moved further along the path. "I'm going to enjoy killing you. I've always hated you. Your smug arrogance. The way you're content to just be a teacher. You haven't any ambition. Well, I do. I'm not going to stay in this stinking city all my life. Sure, I found out Chipper killed his old man and I used it to force Susan. She'd get the money. I'd get the story. I needed this break. I'm tired of covering school committee meetings and writing about people like you. I deserve better."

"My birthmark. I should've figured it out. The year we played basketball together, right? But why did Susan write about me in her diary?"

"See. You're not as smart as you think you are. Susan never kept a diary. I made her do it. We back-dated it. If things went wrong I knew the cops would get their hands on it. I needed someone else we could accuse. You were perfect. So close to Petey. Someone Susan could be seen in public with. All she had to do was say she was concerned about Petey and you'd run out to meet her. The birthmark made it even better. Don't you see, no one showed me the diary. I didn't have to see it. Hell, I helped her write it."

"It doesn't make sense. If Susan was arrested for trying to blackmail McKinley, she would have implicated you. She wouldn't have kept her mouth shut."

"She had no choice. I would have told the cops about her killer brother. I convinced her she could turn state's evidence. Cop a plea and testify you made her do it. She wouldn't have served any jail time, but you would have. Especially when I said Susan told me the whole story. For insurance, I made Susan tell her friends you two were dating."

I wanted to keep him talking. Maybe I'd get a chance to overpower him. I took a step toward him. "You knew Chipper's name was mentioned in the video. You hadn't had time to edit it out. You didn't know how much he knew and you thought the cops might figure out he was alive. How did Susan know Petey was at Walden?"

"Petey went to Walden a lot. We had staked it out Thursday night, but he didn't show. When he called on Friday to say he was all right, Susan knew he was close. She called me and we came out to check. I needed to get that video back."

"Well the cops have it now. They'll figure out who Chipper is."

"That's enough."

"No. That's not enough. Susan met Lois McKinley and was having second thoughts. You knew you had to kill her. You wanted to frame Petey so you took his Medallion. Then when you saw me, you figured that was even better. Everything went your way until now."

I heard footsteps as Aaron started to make his way down the slope.

"Turn around, you bastard."

"You figured I knew where Petey was all the time. Maybe I had the video. You broke into my place looking for it."

"Nice story, Asher. Too bad you're not going to be around to tell it to anyone. The investigation's over. Lois McKinley's family saw to that when I tipped them that the press was onto her love affair with Susan. They didn't want the papers to print their daughter was bisexual."

I sighed. "You figured McKinley was going to keep looking until he found out the truth so you killed him and framed Saulnier. Shit, I should have known something was wrong when you kept leaving the headquarters to have a cigarette. You're not a chain-smoker." I shook my head. "It didn't matter to you that innocent people might die, did it?"

"Which brings the story around to you." he said.

"Right. When I told you Beth and I had gone to Northampton you knew we were looking for Chipper so we had to be stopped." I could hear Aaron's breathing get closer. The flash from his light seemed to float on the water. I had to time things perfectly. "I figured it out. So will the cops."

He didn't say anything. I turned my head for an instant, he was only about twenty-five feet away. "Chipper knows about you," I said. "He's in Waltham. If anything happens to us he'll tell the cops."

"Chipper thinks Molly did his sister. Cop I know told me why they're watching her house."

The flash of his light moved and I knew he was circling, trying to get a better shot. If I charged now he'd get one shot off. Maybe it would go wild. Maybe I could reach him before he fired. I wanted to move, but my feet felt stuck in the sand.

I turned and took a step toward him. "Put down the gun. For Chrissake, how far can you take this. Let us go. Beth and I will never tell."

He sighed. "Don't talk to me like I'm one of your students. I know you too well. You want Susan's killer punished. You'll talk."

I took another step in his direction. I was within a few feet of him. "But Beth won't. Let her go."

I could hear Beth breathing behind me. "Watch out, Steve," she said.

Aaron looked at her. In that split second I lowered my shoulder and charged toward him. I hit him solidly in the chest. He flailed his arms. I brought my knee up between his legs. He doubled over and the gun flew out of his hands. I scrambled across the sand and picked it up.

Aaron slowly straightened. He took several quick breaths. "You don't even know how to use that thing, do you?" He took a step toward me.

I looked at the gun.

The light was sudden and blinding. It came from the path above us. "Hands up. Hands up. Hands up, now," a voice screamed.

Footsteps clomped down the hill. Rita Dooley crouched low, keeping her gun pointed at Aaron. Hollowell was right behind her.

I dropped the gun and raced toward Beth. "Honey, are you all right?"

She smiled slightly, but her eyes were glazed like she was going to pass out.

"She needs an ambulance," I said.

Rita nodded.

More lights came up the path and three officers raced down the hill. Hollowell slipped handcuffs onto Aaron's wrists.

I sat in the sand with my arm around Beth. She rested her head on my shoulder.

Rita talked briefly to the other cops, then walked toward us. She crouched down and examined the bruises on Beth's face. "An ambulance is on the way."

"How the hell did you know?" I said.

Rita straightened and watched as Aaron was led along the path. Then she refocused on me. "When you called I could tell by your voice something was wrong. I figured you might be up to something so I tailed you. I know how you like churches and when you went into the lot I figured you were going to say a few prayers before the committee meeting. I went to the meeting and when you didn't show up I got worried. I grabbed Hollowell and we came out."

Rita walked over to the gun, picked it up, then looked at me. "Could you have shot him?"

"Probably not, but I would have beat the shit out of him with it."

The paramedics examined Beth. Then they put her on a stretcher and carried her to an ambulance. I hopped in back. Her eyes opened as I held her hand.

"He called. Said he had something important to tell me about you." She hesitated and took a long breath. "I shouldn't have let him in."

"Not now, honey," I said. "We can talk later."

She squeezed my hand.

We sat in silence as the ambulance sped down Route 2, then I said, "What're you doing for Thanksgiving?"

"Probably eating turkey through a straw."

"You wanna eat at my place? My turkey will probably taste better that way anyway."

It was Wednesday before I got back to school. All tests done on Beth had been negative, but doctors felt she might have a slight concussion from the fall she took when Aaron hit her in the living room. They were keeping her one more night for observation. I was picking her up at the hospital on Thanksgiving morning. She agreed to spend a couple of weeks at my place. "Just until I'm feeling better," she said. It's a start.

The school committee had called a special meeting on Tuesday night and had rescinded its decision to suspend me, "with apologies." Whatever that meant.

Petey was back with his family. I had talked with him several times and he was looking forward to getting back to school.

Chipper had disappeared again.

My first class of students walked in around eight-ten. They entered quietly and took their seats. The Fleming story had been widely reported and they knew about my involvement in it. Their eyes followed me as I walked to the blackboard.

I picked up a piece of chalk, wrote Henry David Thoreau and underlined it. Then I turned. "Thoreau said, 'The mass of men lead lives of quiet desperation,' and we sometimes lose sight of the things that are really important. He said we glimpse 'higher laws' only on rare occasions. I want to tell you a story about what happened to me at Walden. It began when my phone rang at two o'clock in the morning...."